By John Fante

FICTION

The Saga of Arturo Bandini:
Wait Until Spring, Bandini (1938, 1983)
The Road to Los Angeles (1985)
Ask the Dust (1939, 1980)
Dreams from Bunker Hill (1982)

Dago Red (1940, 1985)
Full of Life (1952, 1988)
The Brotherhood of the Grape (1977, 1988)
The Wine of Youth: Selected Stories of John Fante (1985)
1933 Was a Bad Year (1985)
West of Rome (1986)

LETTERS

*John Fante & H. L. Mencken: A Personal Correspondence
1930-1952* (1989)
Selected Letters 1932–1981 (1991)

John Fante

The Road to Los Angeles

Black Sparrow Press
Santa Rosa — 1996

LIBRARY OF CONGRESS CATALOGING IN PUBLICATION DATA

Fante, John, 1909-1983
   The road to Los Angeles.

   I. Title.
PS3511.A594R6   1985   813'.52   85-15098
ISBN 0-87685-649-0 (pbk.)
ISBN 0-87685-650-4 (hard)

sixth printing

EDITORIAL NOTE

In 1933, John Fante was living in an attic apartment in Long Beach and working on his first novel, *The Road to Los Angeles.* "I have seven months and 450 bucks to write my novel with. This is pretty swell in my opinion," Fante wrote in a letter to Carey McWilliams dated February 23, 1933. Fante had signed a contract with Knopf and received an advance. However, Fante didn't finish the novel in seven months. Sometime during 1936, he reworked the first 100 pages, shortening the book somewhat, and completed the novel. In an undated letter (c. 1936) to McWilliams, Fante writes, "*The Road to Los Angeles* is finished and boy! I'm pleased. . . . I hope to mail it on Friday. Some of the stuff will singe the hair off a wolf's rear. It may be too strong; i.e., lacking in 'good' taste. But that doesn't bother me." The novel was never published, probably because the subject matter was considered too provocative in the mid-1930s.

This novel introduces Fante's alter ego Arturo Bandini who reappears in *Wait Until Spring, Bandini* (1938), *Ask the Dust* (1939), and *Dreams from Bunker Hill* (1982). The manuscript was discovered among John Fante's papers after his death in May, 1983 by his widow Joyce, and now may be included in that short, distinguished list of important first novels by American authors.

J. C.

The Road to Los Angeles

ONE

I had a lot of jobs in Los Angeles Harbor because our family was poor and my father was dead. My first job was ditchdigging a short time after I graduated from high school. Every night I couldn't sleep from the pain in my back. We were digging an excavation in an empty lot, there wasn't any shade, the sun came straight from a cloudless sky, and I was down in that hole digging with two huskies who dug with a love for it, always laughing and telling jokes, laughing and smoking bitter tobacco.

I started with a fury and they laughed and said I'd learn a thing or two after a while. Then the pick and shovel got heavy. I sucked broken blisters and hated those men. One noon I was tired and sat down and looked at my hands. I said to myself, why don't you quit this job before it kills you?

I got up and speared my shovel into the ground.

"Boys," I said. "I'm through. I've decided to accept a job with the Harbor Commission."

Next I was a dishwasher. Every day I looked out a hole of a window, and through it I saw heaps of garbage day after day, with flies droning, and I was like a housewife over a pile of dishes, my hands revolting when I looked down at them swimming like dead fish in the bluish water. The fat cook was the boss. He banged pans and made me work. It made me happy when a fly landed on his big cheek and refused to leave. I had that job four weeks. Arturo, I said, the future of this job is very limited; why don't you quit tonight? Why don't you tell that cook to screw himself?

I couldn't wait until night. In the middle of that August afternoon, with a mountain of unwashed dishes before me, I took off my apron. I had to smile.

"What's funny?" the cook said.

"I'm through. Finished. That's what's funny."

I went out the back door, a bell tinkling. He stood scratching his head in the midst of garbage and dirty dishes. When I thought of all those dishes I laughed, it always seemed so funny.

I became a flunkie on a truck. All we did was move boxes of toilet tissue from the warehouse to the harbor grocery stores in San Pedro and Wilmington. Big boxes, three feet square and weighing fifty pounds apiece. At night I lay in bed thinking about it and tossing.

My boss drove the truck. His arms were tattooed. He wore tight yellow polo shirts. His muscles bulged. He caressed them like a girl's hair. I wanted to say things that would make him writhe. The boxes were piled in the warehouse, fifty feet to the ceiling. The boss folded his arms and had me bring boxes down to the truck. He stacked them. Arturo, I said, you've got to make a decision; he looks tough, but what do you care?

That day I fell down and a box bashed me in the stomach. The boss grunted and shook his head. He made me think of a college football player, and lying on the ground I wondered why he didn't wear a monogram on his chest. I got up smiling. At noon I ate lunch slowly, with a pain where the box bashed me. It was cool under the trailer and I was lying there. The lunch hour passed quickly. The boss came out of the warehouse and saw my teeth inside a sandwich, the peach for dessert untouched at my side.

"I ain't paying you to sit in the shade," he said.

I crawled out and stood up. The words were there, ready. "I'm quitting," I said. "You and your stupid muscles can go to hell. I'm through."

"Good," he said. "I hope so."

"I'm through."

"Thank God for that."

"There's one other thing."

"What?"

"In my opinion you're an overgrown sonofabitch."

He didn't catch me.

After that I wondered what had happened to the peach. I wondered if he had stepped on it with his heel. Three days passed and I went down to find out. The peach lay untouched at the side of the road, a hundred ants feasting upon it.

Then I got a job as a grocery clerk. The man who ran the store was an Italian with a belly like a bushel basket. When Tony Romero was not busy he stood over the cheese bin breaking off little pieces with his fingers. He had a good business. The harbor people traded at his store when they wanted imported food.

One morning he waddled in and saw me with a pad and pencil. I was taking inventory.

"Inventory," he said. "What's that?"

I told him, but he didn't like it. He looked around. "Get to work," he said. "I thought I told you to sweep the floor the first thing every morning."

"You mean you don't want me to take inventory?"

"No. Get to work. No inventory."

Every day at three there was a great rush of customers. It was too much work for one man. Tony Romero worked hard but he waddled, his neck floated in sweat, and people went away because they couldn't waste time waiting. Tony couldn't find me. He hurried to the rear of the store and pounded the bathroom door. I was reading Nietzsche, memorizing a long passage about voluptuousness. I heard the banging on the door but ignored it. Tony Romero put an egg crate in front of the door. and stood on it. His big jaw pushed over the top and looking down he saw me on the other side.

"*Mannaggia Jesu Christi!*" he yelled. "Come out!"

I told him I'd come out immediately. He went away roaring. But I wasn't fired for that.

One night he was checking the day's receipts at the cash

register. It was late, almost nine o'clock. I wanted to get to the library before it closed. He cursed under his breath and called me. I walked over.

"I'm short ten dollars."

I said, "That's funny."

"It's not here."

I checked his figures carefuly three times. The ten was indeed missing. We examined the floor, kicking sawdust around. Then we looked through the cash drawer again, finally taking it out and looking inside the shaft. We couldn't find it. I told him maybe he had given it to somebody by mistake. He was certain he hadn't. He ran his fingers in and out the pockets of his shirt. They were like frankfurters. He patted his pockets.

"Gimme a cigarette."

I pulled a pack from my back pocket, and with it came the ten dollar bill. I had wadded it inside the cigarette pack, but it had worked itself loose. It fell on the floor between us. Tony crushed his pencil until it splintered. His face purpled, his cheeks puffed in and out. He drew back his neck and spat in my face.

"You dirty rat! Get out!"

"Okay," I said. "Suit yourself about that."

I got my Nietzsche book from under the counter and started for the door. Nietzsche! What did he know about Friedrich Nietzsche? He wadded the ten dollar bill and threw it at me. "Your wages for three days, you thief!" I shrugged. Nietzsche in a place like this!

"I'm leaving," I said. "Don't get excited."

"Get out of here!"

He was a good fifty feet away.

"Listen," I said. "I'm tickled to be leaving. I'm sick of your drooling, elephantine hypocrisy. I've been wanting to abandon this preposterous job for a week. So go straight to hell, you Dago fraud!"

I stopped running when I reached the library. It was a

branch of the Los Angeles Public Library. Miss Hopkins was on duty. Her blonde hair was long and combed tightly. I always thought of putting my face in it for the scent. I wanted to feel it in my fists. But she was so beautiful I could hardly talk to her. She smiled. I was out of breath and I glanced at the clock.

"I didn't think I'd make it," I said.

She told me I still had a few minutes. I glanced over the desk and was glad she wore a loose dress. If I could get her to walk across the room on some pretext I might be lucky and see her legs moving in silhouette. I always wondered what her legs were like under glistening hose. She wasn't busy. Only two old people were there, reading newspapers. She checked in the Nietzsche while I got my breath.

"Will you show me the history section?" I said.

She smiled that she would, and I followed. It was a disappointment. The dress was the wrong kind, a light blue; the light didn't penetrate. I watched the curve of her heels. I felt like kissing them. At History she turned and sensed I'd been thinking of her deeply. I felt the cold go through her. She went back to the desk. I pulled out books and put them back again. She still felt my thoughts, but I didn't want to think of anything else. Her legs were crossed under the desk. They were wonderful. I wanted to hug them.

Our eyes met and she smiled, with a smile that said: go ahead and look if you like; there's nothing I can do about it, although I'd like to slap your face. I wanted to talk to her. I could quote her some swell things from Nietzsche; that passage from Zarathustra on voluptuousness. Ah! But I could never quote that one.

She rang the bell at nine. I hurried over to Philosophy and grabbed anything. It was another Nietzsche: *Man and Superman*. I knew that would get her. Before stamping it, she flipped a few pages.

"My!" she said. "What books you read!"

13

I said, "Haw. That's nothing. I never read folderol."

She smiled good night and I said, "It's a magnificent night, ethereally magnificent."

"Is it?" she said.

She gave me an odd look, the pencil point in her hair. I backed out, falling through the door and catching myself. I felt worse outside because it wasn't a magnificent night but cold and foggy, the street lamps hazy in the mist. A car with a man at the wheel and the engine running was at the curb. He was waiting to take Miss Hopkins back to Los Angeles. I thought he looked like a moron. Had he read Spengler? Did he know the West was declining? What was he doing about it? Nothing! He was a boob and a bounder. Nuts to him.

The fog wove around me, soaking into me as I walked along with a cigarette burning. I stopped at Jim's Place on Anaheim. A man was eating at the counter. I had seen him often on the docks. He was a stevedore named Hayes. I sat near him and ordered dinner. While it was cooking I went to the book-stand and looked over the books. They were dollar reprints. I pulled out five. Then I went to the magazine stand and looked at *Artists and Models.* I found two in which the women wore the least clothes and when Jim brought my dinner I told him to wrap them up. He saw the Nietzsche under my arm: *Man and Superman.*

"No," I said. "I'll carry it as it is."

I put it on the counter with a bang. Hayes glanced at the book and read the title: *Man and Superman.* I could see him looking at me through the plate mirror. I was eating my steak. Jim was watching my jaws to find out if the steak was tender. Hayes still stared at the book.

I said, "Jim, this pabulum is indeed antediluvian."

Jim asked what I meant and Hayes stopped eating to listen. "The steak," I said. "It's archaic, primeval, paleoanthropic, and antique. In short, it is senile and aged."

Jim smiled that he didn't understand and the stevedore stopped chewing he was so interested.

"What's that?" Jim said.

"The meat, my friend. The meat. This pabulum before me. It's tougher than a bitch wolf."

When I glanced at Hayes he ducked his head away quickly. Jim was upset about the steak and leaned forward on the counter and whispered he would be glad to cook me another.

I said, "Zounds! Let it go, man! It supersedes my most vaunted aspirations."

I could see Hayes studying me through the mirror. He occupied himself between me and the book. *Man and Superman.* I chewed and stared straight ahead, not paying any attention. All through the meal he watched me intently. Once he stared fixedly at the book for a long time. *Man and Superman.*

When Hayes finished he went to the front to pay his bill. He and Jim stood whispering at the cash register. Hayes nodded. Jim grinned and they whispered again. Hayes smiled and said goodnight, taking a last look at me over his shoulder. Jim came back.

He said, "That fellow wanted to know all about you."

"Indeed!"

"He said you talked like a pretty smart fellow."

"Indeed! Who is he, and what does he do?"

Jim said he was Joe Hayes, the stevedore.

"A poltroonish profession," I said. "Infested by donkeys and boobs. We live in a world of polecats and anthropoids."

I pulled out the ten dollar bill. He brought back the change. I offered him a twenty-five cent tip but he wouldn't take it. "A haphazard gesture," I said. "A mere symbol of fellowship. I like the way you do things, Jim. It strikes an approving note."

"I try to please everybody."

"Well, I'm devoid of complaints, as Chekhov might say."

"What kind of cigarettes do you smoke?"

15

I told him. He got me two packages.
"On me," he said.
I put them in my pocket.
But he wouldn't take a tip.
"Take it!" I said. "It's just a gesture."
He refused. We said goodnight. He walked to the kitchen with the dirty plates and I started for the front. At the door I reached out and grabbed two candy bars from the rack and shoved them under my shirt. The fog swallowed me. I ate the candy walking home. I was glad of the fog because Mr. Hutchins didn't see me. He was standing in the door of his little radio shop. He was looking for me. I owed him four installments on our radio. He could have reached out and touched me but he didn't see me at all.

TWO

We lived in an apartment house next door to a place where a lot of Filipinos lived. The Filipino influx was seasonal. They came south for the fishing season and went back north for the fruit and lettuce seasons around Salinas. There was one family of Filipinos in our house, directly below us. It was a two story pink stucco place with big slabs of stucco wiped from the walls by earthquakes. Every night the stucco absorbed the fog like a blotter. In the mornings the walls were a damp red instead of pink. I liked the red best.

The stairs squealed like a nest of mice. Our apartment was the last on the second floor. As soon as I touched the door knob I felt low. Home always did that to me. Even when my father was alive and we lived in a real house I didn't like it. I always wanted to get away from it, or change it. I used to wonder what home would be like if it was different, but I never could figure out what to do to make it different.

I opened the door. It was dark, the darkness smelling of home, the place where I lived. I turned on the lights. My mother was lying on the divan and the light was waking her up. She rubbed her eyes and got up to her elbows. Every time I saw her half awake it made me think of the times when I was a kid and used to go to her bed in the mornings and smell her asleep until I grew older and couldn't go to her in the mornings because it reminded me too much that she was my mother. It was a salty oily odor. I couldn't even think about her getting older. It burned me up. She sat up and smiled at me, her hair mussed from sleep. Everything she did reminded me of the days when I lived in a real house.

"I thought you'd never get here," she said.

I said, "Where's Mona?"

My mother said she was at church and I said, "My own sister reduced to the superstition of prayer! My own flesh and blood. A nun, a god-lover! What barbarism!"

"Don't start that again," she said. "You're nothing but a boy who's read too many books."

"That's what you think," I said. "It's quite evident that you have a fixation complex."

Her face whitened.

"A what?"

I said, "Forget it. No use talking to yokels, clodhoppers and imbeciles. The intelligent man makes certain reservations as to the choice of his listeners."

She pushed back her hair with long fingers like Miss Hopkins's but they were worn with knobs and wrinkles at the joints, and she wore a wedding ring.

"Are you aware of the fact," I said, "that a wedding ring is not only vulgarly phallic but also the vestigial remains of a primitive savagery anomalous to this age of so-called enlightenment and intelligence?"

She said, "What?"

"Never mind. The feminine mind would not grasp it, even if I explained."

I told her to laugh if she felt like it but some day she would change her tune, and I took my new books and magazines to my private study, which was the clothes closet. There was no electric light in it, so I used candles. There was a feeling in the air that someone or something had been in the study while I was away. I looked around, and I was right, for my sister's little pink sweater hung from one of the clothes hooks.

I lifted it off the hook and said to it, "What do you mean by hanging there? By what authority? Don't you realize you have invaded the sanctity of the house of love?" I opened the door and threw the sweater on the divan.

"No clothes allowed in this room!" I yelled.

My mother came in a hurry. I closed the door and flipped the lock. I could hear her footsteps. The door knob rattled. I started unwrapping the package. The pictures in *Artists and Models* were honeys. I picked my favorite. She was lying on a white rug, holding a red rose to her cheek. I set the picture between the candles on the floor and got down on my knees. "Chloe," I said, "I worship you. Thy teeth are like a flock of sheep on Mount Gilead, and thy cheeks are comely. I am thy humble servant, and I bringeth love everlasting."

"Arturo!" my mother said. "Open up."

"What do you want?"

"What're you doing?"

"Reading. Perusing! Am I denied even that in my own home?"

She rattled the buttons of the sweater against the door. "I don't know what to do with this," she said. "You've got to let me have this clothes closet."

"Impossible."

"What're you doing?"

"Reading."

"Reading what?"

"Literature!"

She wouldn't go away. I could see her toes under the door crack. I couldn't talk to the girl with her standing out there. I put the magazine aside and waited for her to go away. She wouldn't. She didn't even move. Five minutes passed. The candle spluttered. The smoke was filling the place again. She hadn't moved an inch. Finally I set the magazine on the floor and covered it with a box. I felt like yelling at my mother. She could at least move, make a noise, lift her foot, whistle. I picked up a fiction book and stuck my finger in it, as if marking the place. When I opened the door she glared at my face. I had a feeling she knew all about me. She put her hands on her hips and sniffed at the air. Her eyes looked everywhere, the corners, the ceiling, the floor.

"What on earth are you doing in there?"

"Reading! Improving my mind. Do you forbid even that?"

"There's something awfully strange about this," she said. "Are you reading those nasty picture books again?"

"I'll have no Methodists, prudes, or pruriency in my house. I'm sick of this polecat wowserism. The awful truth is that my own mother is a smut hound of the worst type."

"They make me sick," she said.

I said, "Don't blame the pictures. You're a Christian, an Epworth Leaguer, a Bible-Belter. You're frustrated by your brummagem Christianity. You're at heart a scoundrel and a jackass, a bounder and an ass."

She pushed me aside and walked into the closet. Inside was the odor of burning wax and brief passions spent on the floor. She knew what the darkness held. Then she ran out.

"God in heaven!" she said. "Let me out of here." She pushed me aside and slammed the door. I heard her banging pots and pans in the kitchen. Then the kitchen door slammed. I locked the door and went back to the picture and lit the candles. After a while my mother knocked and told me supper was ready. I told her I had eaten. She hovered at the door. She was getting annoyed again. I could feel it coming on. There was a chair at the door. I heard her drag it into position and sit down. I knew she sat with folded arms, looking at her shoes, her feet straight out in that characteristic way she had of sitting and waiting. I closed the magazine and waited. If she could stand it I could too. Her toe beat a tap on the carpet. The chair squeaked. The beat increased. All at once she jumped up and started hammering the door. I opened it in a hurry.

"Come out of there!" she screamed.

I got out as fast as I could. She smiled, tired but relieved. She had small teeth. One below was out of line like a soldier out of step. She wasn't more than five three but she looked tall when she had on high heels. Her aged showed most in her skin. She was forty-five. Her skin sagged some under the ears. I was glad her hair wasn't grey. I always looked for grey hairs but didn't find any. I pushed her and tickled her and she laughed and fell into the chair. Then I went to the divan and stretched out and slept awhile.

THREE

My sister woke me up when she got home. I had a headache and there was a pain like a sore muscle in my back and I knew what that was from — thinking too much about naked women. It was eleven o'clock by the clock on the radio. My sister took off her coat and started for the clothes closet. I told her to stay out of there or get killed. She smiled superciliously and carried her coat to the bedroom. I rolled over and threw my feet on the floor. I asked her where she'd been but she didn't answer. She always got my goat because she seldom paid any attention to me. I didn't hate her but sometimes I wished I did. She was a pretty kid, sixteen years old. She was a little taller than me, with black hair and eyes. Once she won a contest in high school for having the best teeth. Her rear end was like a loaf of Italian bread, round and just right. I used to see fellows looking at it and I know it got them. But she was cold and the way she walked was deceptive. She didn't like a fellow to look at her. She thought it was sinful; anyhow she said so. She said it was nasty and shameful.

When she left the bedroom door open I used to watch her, and sometimes I peeked through the keyhole or hid under the bed. She would stand with her back to the mirror and examine her bottom, running her hands over it and pulling her dress around it tightly. She wouldn't wear a dress that didn't fit her tightly around the waist and hips and she was always brushing off the chair before she sat down. Then she sat down primly but in a cold way. I tried to get her to smoke cigarettes but she wouldn't. I also tried to advise her on life and sex but she thought I was crazy. She was like my father had been, very clean and a hard worker at school and home. She bossed my mother. She was smarter than my mother, but I didn't think she could ever approach my mind for sheer brilliance. She bossed everybody but me. After my father died she tried to boss me too. I wouldn't think of it, my own sister, and so she decided I wasn't worth bossing anyhow. Once in a while I let her boss me though, but it was only to exhibit my flexible personality. She was as clean as ice. We fought like cats and dogs.

I had something she didn't like. It repulsed her. I guess she suspected the clothes-closet women. Once in a while, I teased her by patting her rear. She got insanely mad. Once I did it and she got a butcher knife and chased me out of the apartment. She didn't speak for two weeks and she told my mother she'd never speak to me again, or even eat with me at the same table. Finally she got over it, but I never did forget how mad she got. She would have butchered me that time if she had caught me.

She had the same thing my father had, but it was not in

my mother or me. I mean cleanliness. Once when I was a kid I saw a rattlesnake fighting three Scotch terriers. The dogs snatched him from a rock where he was sunning himself, and they tore him to pieces. The snake fought hard, never losing his temper, he knew he was finished, and each of the dogs carried off a dripping hunk of his body. They left only the tail and three rattles, and that part of him still moved. Even after he was in pieces I thought he was a wonder. I went over to the rock, which had some blood on it. I put my finger in the blood and tasted it. I cried like a child. I never forgot him. And yet had he been alive I wouldn't have gone near him. It was something like that with my sister and my father.

I thought as long as my sister was so good-looking and bossy she would make a swell wife. But she was too cold and too religious. Whenever a man came to our house for a date with her, she wouldn't accept. She would stand in the door and not even invite him to come in. She wanted to be a nun, that was the trouble. What kept her from it was my mother. She was waiting a few more years. She said the only man she loved was the Son of Man, and the only bridegroom for her was Christ. It sounded like stuff from the nuns. Mona couldn't think things like that without outside help.

Her grade school days were spent with the nuns in San Pedro. When she graduated my father couldn't afford sending her to a Catholic high school, so she went to Wilmington High. As soon as it was over she started going back to San Pedro to visit the nuns. She stayed all day, helping them correct papers, giving kindergarten lessons and things like that. In the evenings she fooled around the Church on the Wilmington side of the harbor, decorating the altars with all kinds of flowers. She'd been doing that tonight.

She came out of the bedroom in her robe.

I said, "How's Jehovah tonight? What does He think of the quantum theory?"

She went into the kitchen and started talking to my mother about the church. They argued about flowers, which was best for the altar, red or white roses.

I said, "Yahweh. Next time you see Yahweh tell him I have a few questions to ask."

They kept on talking.

"Oh Lord Holy Jehovah, behold your sanctimonious and worshipful Mona at your feet, drooling idiotic persiflage. Oh Jesus, she's holy. Sweet jumping Jesus Christ, she's sacred."

My mother said, "Arturo, stop that. Your sister's tired."

"Oh Holy Ghost, Oh holy inflated triple ego, get us out of the Depression. Elect Roosevelt. Keep us on the gold standard. Take France off, but for Christ's sake keep us on!"

"Arturo, stop that."

"Oh Jehovah, in your infinite mutability see if you can't scrape up some coin for the Bandini family."

My mother said, "Shame, Arturo. Shame."

I got up on the divan and yelled, "I reject the hypothesis of God! Down with the decadence of a fraudulent Christianity! Religion is the opium of the people! All that we are or ever hope to be we owe to the devil and his bootleg apples!"

My mother came after me with the broom. She almost stumbled over it, threatening me with the straw end in my face. I pushed the broom aside and jumped down on the floor. Then I pulled off my shirt in front of her and stood naked from the waist up. I bent my neck toward her.

"Vent your intolerance," I said. "Persecute me! Put me on the rack! Express your Christianity! Let the Church Militant display its bloody soul! Gibbet me! Stick hot pokers in my eyes. Burn me at the stake, you Christian dogs!"

Mona came in with a glass of water. She took the broom away from my mother and gave her the water. My mother drank it and calmed down a bit. Then she spluttered and coughed into the glass and was ready to cry.

"Mother!" Mona said. "Don't cry. He's nutty."

She looked at me with a waxy, expressionless face. I turned my back and walked to the window. When I turned around she was still staring.

"Christian dogs," I said. "Bucolic rainspouts! Boobus Americanus! Jackals, weasels, polecats, and donkeys — the whole stupid lot of you. I alone of the entire family have been unmarked by the scourge of cretinism."

"You fool," she said.

They walked into the bedroom.

"Don't call me a fool," I said. "You neurosis! You frustrated, inhibited, driveling, drooling, half-nun!"

My mother said, "Did you hear that! How awful!"

They went to bed. I had the divan and they had the bedroom. When their door closed I got out the magazines and piled into bed. I was glad to be able to look at the girls under the lights of the big room. It was a lot better than that smelly closet. I talked to them about an hour, went into the mountains with Elaine, and to the South Seas with Rosa, and finally in a group meeting with all of them spread around me, I told them I played no favorites and that each in her turn would get her chance. But after a while I got awfully tired of it, for I got to feeling more and more like an idiot until I began to hate the idea that they were only pictures, flat and single-faced and so alike in color and smile. And they all smiled like whores. It all got very hateful and I thought, Look at yourself! Sitting here and talking to a lot of prostitutes. A fine superman *you* turned out to be! What if Nietzsche could see you now? And Schopenhauer — what would he think? And Spengler! Oh, would Spengler roar at you! You fool, you idiot, you swine, you beast, you rat, you filthy, contemptible, disgusting little swine! Suddenly I grabbed the pictures up in a batch and tore them to pieces and threw them down the bowl in the bathroom. Then I crawled back to bed and kicked the covers off. I hated myself so much that I sat up in bed thinking the worst possible things about myself. Finally I was so despicable there was nothing left to do but sleep. It was hours before I dozed off. The fog was thinning in the east and the west was black and grey. It must have been three o'clock. From the bedroom I heard my mother's soft snores. By then I was ready to commit suicide, and so thinking I fell asleep.

FOUR

At six my mother got up and called me. I rolled around and didn't want to get up. She took the bedclothes and tossed them back. It left me naked on the sheet because I didn't sleep wearing anything. That was all right, but it was morning and I wasn't prepared for it, and she could see it, and I didn't mind her seeing me naked but not the way a fellow will be some times in the morning. I put my hand over the place and tried to hide it, but she saw anyway. It seemed she was deliberately looking for something to embarrass me — my own mother, too.

She said, "Shame on you, early in the morning."

"Shame on me?" I said. "How come?"

"Shame on you."

"Oh God, what'll you Christians think of next! Now it's shameful to even be asleep!"

"You know what I mean," she said. "Shame on you, a boy your age. Shame on you. Shame. Shame."

"Well, shame on you too, for that matter. And shame on Christianity."

She went back to bed.

"Shame on him," she said to Mona.

"What'd he do now?"

"Shame on him."

"What did he do?"

"Nothing, but shame on him anyway. Shame."

I fell asleep. After a while she called again.

"I'm not going to work this morning," I said.

"Why not?"

"I lost my job."

A dead silence. Then she and Mona sat up in bed. My job meant everything. We still had Uncle Frank, but they figured my earnings before that. I had to think of something good, because they both knew I was a liar. I could fool my mother but Mona never believed anything, not even the truth if I spoke it.

I said, "Mr. Romero's nephew just arrived from the old country. He got my job."

"I hope you don't expect us to believe *that!*" Mona said.

"My expectations scarcely concern imbeciles," I said.

My mother came to the bed. The story wasn't very convincing but she was willing to give me the breaks. If Mona hadn't been there it would have been a cinch. She told Mona to keep still and listened for more. Mona was messing it up by talking. I yelled at her to shut up.

My mother said, "Are you telling the truth?"

I put my hand over my heart and closed my eyes and said, "Before Almighty God and his heavenly court I solemnly swear that I am neither lying or elaborating. If I am, I hope He strikes me dead this very minute. Get the clock."

She got the clock off the radio. She believed in miracles, any kind of miracles. I closed my eyes and felt my heart pounding. I held my breath. The moments passed. After a minute I let the air out of my lungs. My mother smiled and kissed me on the forehead. But now she blamed Romero.

"He can't do this to you," she said. "I won't let him. I'm going down and give him a piece of my mind."

I jumped out of bed. I was naked but I didn't care. I said, "God Almighty! Haven't you any pride, any sense of human dignity? Why should you see him after he treated me with such levantine scurrilousness? Do you want to disgrace the family name too?"

She was dressing in the bedroom. Mona laughed and fingered her hair. I went in and pulled off my mother's stockings and tied them in knots before she could stop me. Mona shook her head and tittered. I put my fist under her nose and gave her a final warning not to butt in. My mother didn't know what to do next. I put my hands on her shoulders and looked into her eyes. "I am a man of deep pride," I said. "Does that strike an approving chord in your sense of judgment? Pride! My first and last utterance rises from the soul of that stratum I call Pride. Without it my life is a lusty disillusionment. In short, I am delivering you an ultimatum. If you go down to Romero's I'll kill myself."

That scared the devil out of her, but Mona rolled over and laughed and laughed. I didn't say more but went back to bed and pretty soon I fell asleep.

When I woke up it was around noon and they were gone somewhere. I got out the picture of an old girl of mine I called Marcella and we went to Egypt and made love in a slave-driven boat on the Nile. I drank wine from her sandals and milk from her breasts and then we had the slaves paddle us to the river bank and I fed her hearts of hummingbirds seasoned in sweetened pigeon milk. When it was over I felt like the devil. I felt like hitting myself in the nose, knocking myself unconscious. I wanted to cut myself, to feel my bones cracking. I tore the picture of Marcella to pieces and got rid of it and then I went to the medicine cabinet and got a razor blade, and before I knew it I slit my arm below the elbow, but not deeply so that it was only blood and no pain. I sucked the slit but there was still no pain, so I got some salt and rubbed it in and felt it bite my flesh, hurting me and making me come out of it and feel alive again, and I rubbed it until I couldn't stand it any longer. Then I bandaged my arm.

They had left a note for me on the table. It said they had

gone to Uncle Frank's and that there was food in the pantry for my breakfast. I decided to eat at Jim's Place, because I still had some money. I crossed the schoolyard which was across the street from the apartment and went over to Jim's. I ordered ham and eggs. While I ate Jim talked.

He said, "You read a lot. Did you ever try writing a book?"

That did it. From then on I wanted to be a writer. "I'm writing a book right now," I said.

He wanted to know what kind of a book.

I said, "My prose is not for sale. I write for posterity."

He said, "I didn't know that. What do you write? Stories? Or plain fiction?"

"Both. I'm ambidextrous."

"Oh. I didn't know that."

I went over to the other side of the place and bought a pencil and a notebook. He wanted to know what I was writing now. I said, "Nothing. Merely taking random notes for a future work on foreign trade. The subject interests me curiously, a sort of dynamic hobby I've picked up."

When I left he was staring at me with his mouth open. I took it easy down to the harbor. It was June down there, the best time of all. The mackerel were running off the south coast and the canneries were going full blast, night and day, and all the time at that time of the year there was a stink in the air of putrefaction and fish oil. Some people considered it a stink and some got sick from it, but it was not a stink to me, except the fish smell which was bad, but to me it was great. I liked it down there. It wasn't one smell but a lot of them weaving in and out, so every step you took brought a different odor. It made me dreamy and I did a lot of thinking about far-away places, the mystery of what the bottom of the sea contained, and all the books I'd read came alive at once and I saw better people out of books, like Philip Carey, Eugene Witla, and the fellows Dreiser made.

The Road to Los Angeles

I liked the odor of bilge water from old tankers, the odor of crude oil in barrels bound for distant places, the odor of oil on the water turned slimy and yellow and gold, the odor of rotting lumber and the refuse of the sea blackened by oil and tar, of decayed fruit, of little Japanese fishing sloops, of banana boats and old rope, of tugboats and scrap iron and the brooding mysterious smell of the sea at low tide.

I stopped at the white bridge that crossed the channel to the left of the Pacific Coast Fisheries on the Wilmington side. A tanker was unloading at the gasoline docks. Up the street Jap fishermen were repairing their nets, stretched for blocks along the water's edge. At the American-Hawaiian stevedores were loading a ship for Honolulu. They worked in their bare backs. They looked like something great to write about. I flattened the new notebook against the rail, dipped the pencil on my tongue and started to write a treatise on the stevedore: "A Psychological Interpretation of the Stevedore Today and Yesterday, by Arturo Gabriel Bandini."

It turned out a tough subject. I tried four or five times but gave up. Anyhow, the subject took years of research; there wasn't any need for prose yet. The first thing to do was get my facts together. Maybe it would take two years, three, even four; in fact it was the job of a lifetime, a magnum opus. It was too tough. I gave it up. I figured philosophy was easier.

"A Moral and Philosophical Dissertation on Man and Woman, by Arturo Gabriel Bandini." Evil is for the weak man, so why be weak. It is better to be strong than to be weak, for to be weak is to lack strength. Be strong, my brothers, for I say unless ye be strong the forces of evil shall get ye. All strength is a form of power. All lack of strength is a form of evil. All evil is a form of weakness. Be strong, lest ye be weak. Avoid weakness that ye might become strong. Weakness eateth the heart of woman. Strength feedeth the heart of man. Do ye wish to become females? Aye, then grow weak. Do ye wish to become men? Aye, aye. Then grow strong. Down with Evil! Up with Strength! Oh Zarathustra, endow thy women with plenty of weakness! Oh Zarathustra, endow thy men with plenty of strength! Down with woman! Hail Man!

Then I got tired of the whole thing. I decided maybe I wasn't a writer after all but a painter. Maybe my genius lay in art. I turned a page in the book and figured on doing some sketching just for the practice, but I couldn't find anything worth drawing, only ships and stevedores and docks, and they didn't interest me. I drew cats-on-the-fence, faces, triangles and squares. Then I got the idea I wasn't an artist or a writer but an architect, for my father had been a carpenter and maybe the building trade was more in keeping with my heritage. I drew a few houses. They were about the same, square places with a chimney out of which smoke poured. I put the notebook away.

It was hot on the bridge, the heat stinging the back of my neck. I crawled through the rail to some jagged rocks tumbled about at the edge of the water. They were big rocks, black as coal from immersions at high tide, some of them big as a house. Under the bridge they were scattered in crazy disorder like a field of icebergs, and yet they looked contented and undisturbed.

I crawled under the bridge and I had a feeling I was the only one who had ever done it. The small harbor waves lapped at the rocks and left little pools of green water here and there. Some of the rocks were draped in moss, and others had pretty spots of bird dung. The ponderous odor of the sea came up. Under the girders it was so cold and so dark I couldn't see much. From above I heard the traffic pounding, horns honking, men yelling, and big trucks battering the timber crosspieces. It was such a terrible din that it hammered my ears and when I yelled my voice went out a few feet and rushed back as if fastened to a rubber band. I crawled along the stones until I got out of the range of the sunlight. It was a strange place. For a while I was scared. Farther on there was a great stone, bigger than the rest, its crest ringed with the white dung of gulls. It was the king of all those stones with a crown of white. I started for it.

All of a sudden everything at my feet began to move. It was the quick slimy moving of things that crawled. I caught my breath, hung on, and tried to fix my gaze. They were crabs! The stones were alive and swarming with them. I was so scared I couldn't move and the noise from above was nothing compared to the thunder of my heart.

I leaned against a stone and put my face in my hands until I wasn't afraid. When I took my hands away I could see through the blackness and it was grey and cold, like a world under the earth, a grey, solitary place. For the first time I got a good look at the things living down there. The big crabs were the size of house bricks, silent and cruel as they held forth on top the large stones, their menacing antennae moving sensuously like the arms of a hula dancer, their little eyes mean and ugly. There were a lot more of the smaller crabs, about the size of my hand, and they swam around in the little black pools at the base of the rocks, crawling over one another, pulling one another into the lapping blackness as they fought for positions on the stones. They were having a good time.

There was a nest of even smaller crabs at my feet, each the size of a dollar, a big chunk of squirming legs jumbled together. One of them grabbed my pants cuff. I pulled him off and held him while he clawed helplessly and tried to bite me. I had him though and he was helpless. I pulled back my arm and threw him against a stone. He crackled, smashed to death, stuck for a moment upon the stone, then falling with blood and water exuding. I picked up the smashed shell and tasted the yellow fluid coming from it, which was salty as sea water and I didn't like it. I threw him out to deep water. He floated until a jack smelt swam around him and examined him, and then began to bite him viciously and finally dragged him out of sight, the smelt slithering away. My hands were bloody and sticky and the smell of

31

the sea was on them. All at once I felt a swelling in me to kill these crabs, every one of them.

The small ones didn't interest me, it was the big ones I wanted to kill and kill. The big fellows were strong and ferocious with powerful incisors. They were worthy adversaries for the great Bandini, the conquering Arturo. I looked around but couldn't find a switch or a stick. On the bank against the concrete there was a pile of stones. I rolled up my sleeves and started throwing them at the largest crab I could see, one asleep on a stone twenty feet away. The stones landed all around him, within an inch of him, sparks and chips flying, but he didn't even open his eyes to find out what was going on. I threw about twenty times before I got him. It was a triumph. The stone crushed his back with the sound of a breaking soda cracker. It went clear through him, pinning him to the stone. Then he fell into the water, the foamy green bubbles at the edge swallowing him. I watched him disappear and shook my fist at him, waving angry farewells as he floated to the bottom. Goodbye, goodbye! We will doubtless meet again in another world; you will not forget me, Crab. You will remember me forever and forever as your conqueror!

Killing them with stones was too tough. The stones were so sharp they cut my fingers when I heaved them. I washed the blood and slime off my hands and made my way to the edge again. Then I climbed onto the bridge and walked down the street to a ship chandler's shop three blocks away, where they sold guns and ammunition.

I told the white-faced clerk I wanted to buy an air gun. He showed me a high powered one and I laid the money down and bought it without questions. I spent the rest of the ten on ammunition — BB shot. I was anxious to get back to the battlefield so I told white face not to wrap the ammunition but give it to me like that. He thought that was strange and he looked me over while I scooped the cylinders off the counter and left the shop as fast as I could but not running. When I got outside I started to run, and then I sensed somebody was watching me and I looked around, and sure enough white face was standing in the door and peering after me through the hot afternoon air. I slowed down to a fast walk until I got to the corner and then I started to run again.

I shot crabs all that afternoon, until my shoulder hurt behind the gun and my eyes ached behind the gunsight. I was Dictator Bandini, Ironman of Crabland. This was another Blood Purge for the good of the Fatherland. They had tried to unseat me, those damned crabs, they had had the guts to try to foment a revolution, and I was getting revenge. To think of it! It infuriated me. These goddamned crabs had actually questioned the might of Superman Bandini! What had got into them to be so stupidly presumptuous? Well, they were going to get a lesson they would never forget. This was going to be the last revolution they'd ever attempt, by Christ. I gnashed my teeth when I thought of it — a nation of revolting crabs. What guts! God, I was mad.

I pumped shot until my shoulder ached and a blister rose on my trigger finger. I killed over five hundred and wounded twice as many. They were alive to the attack, insanely angry and frightened as the dead and wounded dropped from the ranks. The siege was on. They swarmed toward me. Others came out of the sea, still others from behind rocks, moving in vast numbers across the plain of stones toward death who sat on a high rock out of their reach.

I gathered some of the wounded into a pool and had a military conference and decided to courtmartial them. I drew them out of the pool one at a time, sitting each over the mouth of the rifle and pulling the trigger. There was one crab, bright colored and full of life who reminded me of a woman: doubtless a princess among the renegades, a brave crabess seriously injured, one of her legs shot away, an arm dangling pitifully. It broke my heart. I had another conference and decided that, due to the extreme urgency of the situation, there must not be any sexual discrimination. Even the princess had to die. It was unpleasant but it had to be done.

With a sad heart I knelt among the dead and dying and invoked God in a prayer, asking that he forgive me for this most beastly of the crimes of a superman—the execution of a woman. And yet, after all, duty was duty, the old order must be preserved, revolution must be stamped out, the regime had to go on, the renegades must perish. For some time I talked to the princess in private, formally extending to her the apologies of the Bandini government, and abiding by her last request—it was that I permit her to hear La Paloma—I whistled it to her with great feeling so that I was crying when finished. I raised my gun to her beautiful face and pulled the trigger. She died instantly, gloriously, a flaming mass of shell and yellowed blood.

Out of sheer reverence and admiration I ordered a stone placed where she had fallen, this ravishing heroine of one of the world's unforgettable revolutions, who had perished during the bloody June days of the Bandini government. History was written that day. I made the sign of the cross over the stone, kissed it reverently, even with a touch of passion, and held my head low in a momentary cessation of attack. It was an ironic moment. For in a flash I realized I had loved that woman. But, on Bandini! The attack began again. Shortly after, I shot down another woman. She was not so seriously injured, she suffered from shock. Taken prisoner, she offered herself to me body and soul. She begged me to spare her life. I laughed fiendishly. She was an exquisite creature, reddish and pink, and only a foregone conclusion as to my destiny made me accept her touching offer. There beneath the bridge in the darkness I ravaged her while she pleaded for mercy. Still laughing I took her out and shot her to pieces, apologizing for my brutality.

The slaughter finally stopped when my head ached from eye strain. Before leaving I took another last look around. The miniature cliffs were smeared with blood. It was a triumph, a very great victory for me. I went among the dead and spoke to them consolingly, for even though they were my enemies I was for all that a man of nobility and I respected them and admired them for the valiant struggle they had offered my legions. "Death has arrived for you," I said. "Goodbye, dear enemies. You were brave in fighting and braver in death, and Führer Bandini has not forgotten. He overtly praises, even in death." To others I said, "Goodbye, thou coward. I spit on thee in disgust. Thy cowardice is repugnant to the Führer. He hateth cowards as he hateth the plague. He will not be reconciled. May the tides of the sea wash thy cowardly crime from the earth, thou knave."

I climbed back to the road just as the six o'clock whistles were blowing, and started for home. There were some kids playing ball in an empty lot up the street, and I gave them the gun and ammunition in exchange for a pocket knife which one kid claimed was worth three dollars, but he didn't fool me, because I knew the knife wasn't worth more than fifty cents. I wanted to get rid of the gun though, so I made the deal. The kids figured I was a sap, but I let them.

FIVE

The apartment smelled of a steak cooking, and in the kitchen I heard them talking. Uncle Frank was there. I looked in and said hello and he said the same. He was sitting with my sister in the breakfast nook. My mother was at the stove. He was my mother's brother, a man of forty-five with grey temples and big eyes and little hairs growing out of his nostrils. He had fine teeth. He was gentle. He lived alone in a cottage across town. He was very fond of Mona and wanted to do things for her all the time but she rarely accepted. He always helped us with money, and after my father died he practically supported us for months. He wanted us to live with him, but I was against it because he could be bossy. When my father died he paid the funeral bill and even bought a stone for the grave, which was unusual because he never thought much of my father for a brother-in-law.

The kitchen overflowed with food. There was a bushel basket of groceries on the floor and the sink board was covered with vegetables. We had a big dinner. They did all the talking. I felt crabs all over me, and in my food. I thought of those living crabs under the bridge, groping in the darkness after their dead. There was that crab Goliath. He had been a great fighter. I remembered his wonderful personality; undoubtedly he had been the leader of his people. Now he was dead. I wondered if his father and mother searched for his body in the darkness and thought of the sadness of his lover, and whether she was dead too. Goliath had fought with slits of hatred in his eyes. It had taken a lot of BB shot to kill him. He was a great crab — the greatest of all contemporary crabs, including the Princess. The Crab People ought to build him a monument. But was he greater than me? No sir. I was his conqueror. To think of it! That mighty crab, hero of his people, and I was his conqueror. The Princess too — the most ravishing crab ever known — and I had killed her too. Those crabs wouldn't forget me for a long time to come. If they wrote history I would get a lot of space in their records. They might even call me the Black Killer of the Pacific Coast. Little crabs would hear about me from their forebears and I would strike terror in their memories. By fear I would rule, even though I was not present, changing the course of their existences. Some day I would become a legend in their world. And there might even be romantic female crabs fascinated by my cruel execution of the Princess. They would make me a god, and some of them would secretly worship me and have a passion for me.

Uncle Frank and my mother and Mona kept on talking. It looked like a plot. Once Mona glanced at me, and her glance said: We are ignoring you deliberately because we want you to be uncomfortable; furthermore, you'll have your hands full with

Uncle Frank after the meal. Then Uncle Frank gave me a loose smile. I knew then it meant trouble.

After the dessert the women got up and left. My mother closed the door. The whole thing looked premeditated. Uncle Frank got down to business by lighting his pipe, pushing some dishes out of the way, and leaning toward me. He took the pipe out of his mouth and shook the stem under my nose.

He said, "Look here, you little sonofabitch; I didn't know you were a thief too. I knew you were lazy, but by God I didn't know you were a thieving little thief."

I said, "I'm not a sonofabitch, either."

"I talked to Romero," he said. "I know what you did."

"I warn you," I said. "In no uncertain terms I warn you to desist from calling me a sonofabitch again."

"You stole ten dollars from Romero."

"Your presumption is colossal, unvaunted. I fail to see why you permit yourself the liberty of insulting me by calling me a sonofabitch."

He said, "Stealing from your employer! That's a fine thing."

"I tell you again, and with utmost candor that, despite your seniority and our blood-relationship, I positively forbid you to use such opprobious names as sonofabitch in reference to me."

"A loafer and a thief for a nephew! It's disgusting."

"Please be advised, my dear uncle, that since you choose to vilify me with sonofabitch I have no alternative but to point out the blood-fact of your own scurrilousness. In short, if I am a sonofabitch it so happens that you're the brother of a bitch. Laugh that off."

"Romero could've had you arrested. I'm sorry he didn't."

"Romero is a monster, a gigantic fraud, a looming lug. His charges of piracy amuse me. I fail to be moved by his sterile accusations. But I must remind you once more to curb the glibness of your obscenities. I am not in the habit of being insulted, even by relatives."

He said, "Shut up, you little fool! I'm talking about something else. What'll you do now?"

"There are myriad possibilities."

He sneered, "Myriad possibilities! That's a good one! What the devil are you talking about? Myriad possibilities!"

I took some puffs on my cigarette and said, "I presume I'll embark on my literary career now that I have had done with the Romero breed of proletarian."

"Your *what*?"

"My literary plans. My prose. I shall continue with my literary efforts. I'm a writer, you know."

"A writer! Since when did you become a writer? This is a new one. Go on, I've never heard this one before."

I told him, "The writing instinct has always lain dormant in me. Now it is in the process of metamorphosis. The era of transition has passed. I am on the threshold of expression."

He said, "Balls."

I took the new notebook out of my pocket and flipped the pages with my thumb. I flipped them so fast he couldn't read anything but he could see some writing in it. "These are notes," I said. "Atmospheric notes. I'm writing a Socratic symposium on Los Angeles Harbor since the days of the Spanish Conquest."

"Let's see them," he said.

"Nothing doing. Not until after publication."

"After publication! What talk!"

I put the notebook back in my pocket. It smelled of crabs.

"Why don't you buck up and be a man?" he said. "It would make your father happy up there."

"Up where?" I said.

"In afterlife."

I'd been waiting for that.

"There is no afterlife," I said. "The celestial hypothesis is sheer propaganda formulated by the haves to delude the have-nots. I dispute the immortal soul. It is the persistent delusion of an hoodwinked mankind. I reject in no uncertain terms the hypothesis of God. Religion is the opium of the people. The churches should be converted to hospitals and public works. All we are or ever hope to be we owe to the devil and his bootleg apples. There are 78,000 contradictions in the bible. Is it God's word? No! I reject God! I denounce him with savage and relentless imprecations! I accept the universe godless. I am a monist!"

"You're crazy," he said. "You're a maniac."

"You don't understand me, " I smiled. "But that's all right. I anticipate misunderstanding; nay, I look forward to the worst persecutions along the way. It's quite all right."

He emptied his pipe and shook his finger under my nose. "The thing for you to do is stop reading all these damn books, stop stealing, make a man out of yourself, and go to work."

I smashed out my cigarette. "Books!" I said. "And what do *you* know about books! You! An ignoramus, a Boobus Americanus, a donkey, a clod-hopping poltroon with no more sense than a polecat."

He kept still and filled his pipe. I didn't say anything because it was his turn. He studied me awhile while he thought of something.

""I've got a job for you," he said.

"What doing?"

"I don't know yet. I'll see."

"It has to fit my talents. Don't forget that I'm a writer. I've metamorphosed."

"I don't care what's happened to you. You're going to work. Maybe the fish canneries."

"I don't know anything about fish canneries."

"Good," he said. "The less you know the better. All it takes is a strong back and a weak mind. You've got both."

"The job doesn't interest me," I told him. "I'd rather write prose."

"Prose — what's prose?"

"You're a bourgeois Babbitt. You'll never know good prose as long as you live."

"I ought to knock your block off."

"Try it."

"You little bastard."

"You American boor."

He got up and left the table with his eyes flashing. Then he went into the next room and talked to Mother and Mona, telling them we had had an understanding and from now on I was turning over a new leaf. He gave them some money and told my mother not to worry about anything. I went to the door and nodded goodnight when he left. My mother and Mona looked at my eyes. They thought I'd come out of the kitchen with tears streaming down my face. My mother put her hands on my shoulders. She was sweet and soothing, thinking Uncle Frank had made me feel miserable.

"He hurt your feelings," she said. "Didn't he, my poor boy."

I pulled her arms off.

"Who?" I said. "That cretin? Hell, no!"

"You look like you've been crying."

I walked into the bedroom and looked at my eyes in the mirror. They were as dry as ever. My mother followed and started to pat them with her handkerchief. I thought, what the heck.

"May I ask what you're doing?" I said.

"You poor boy! It's all right. You're embarrassed. I understand. Mother understands everything."

"But I'm *not* crying!"

She was disappointed and turned away.

SIX

It's morning, time to get up, so get up, Arturo, and look for a job. Get out there and look for what you'll never find. You're a thief and you're a crab-killer and a lover of women in clothes closets. *You'll* never find a job!

Every morning I got up feeling like that. Now I've got to find a job, damn it to hell. I ate breakfast, put a book under my arm, pencils in my pocket, and started out. Down the stairs I went, down the street, sometimes hot and sometimes cold, sometimes foggy and sometimes clear. It never mattered, with a book under my arm, looking for a job.

What job, Arturo? Ho ho! A job for you? Think of what you are, my boy! A crab-killer. A thief. You look at naked women in clothes closets. And *you* expect to get a job! How funny! But there he goes, the idiot, with a big book. Where the devil are you going, Arturo? Why do you go up this street and not that? Why go east — why not go west? Answer me, you thief! Who'll give you a job, you swine — who? But there's a park across town, Arturo. It's called Banning Park. There are a lot of beautiful eucalyptus trees in it, and green lawns. What a place to read! Go there, Arturo. Read Nietzsche. Read Schopenhauer. Get into the company of the mighty. A job? fooey! Go sit under an eucalyptus tree reading a book looking for a job.

And still a few times I did look for a job. There was the fifteen cents store. For a long time I stood out in front looking at a pile of peanut brittle in the window. Then I walked in.

"The manager, please."

The girl said, "He's downstairs."

I knew him. His name was Tracey. I walked down the hard stairs, wondering why they were so hard, and at the bottom I saw Mr. Tracey. He was fixing his yellow tie at a mirror. A nice man, that Mr. Tracey. Admirable taste. A beautiful tie, white shoes, blue shirt. A fine man, a privilege to work for a man like that. He had something; he had *élan vital*. Ah, Bergson! Another great writer was Bergson.

"Hello, Mr. Tracey."

"Eh, what do you want?"

"I was going to ask you—"

"We have application blanks for that. But it won't do any good. We're all filled up."

I went back up the hard stairs. What curious stairs! So hard, so precise! Possibly a new invention in stair-making. Ah, mankind! What'll you think of next! Progress. I believe in the reality of Progress. That Tracey. That lowdown, filthy, no-good sonofabitch! Him and his stupid yellow necktie standing in front of a mirror like a goddamn ape: that bourgeois Babbitt scoundrel. A yellow necktie! Imagine it. Oh, he didn't fool me. I knew a thing or two about that fellow. One night I was there, down at the harbor, and I saw him. I hadn't said anything, but I guess I'd seen him down there in his car, potbellied as a pig, with a girl at his side. I saw his fat teeth in the moonlight. He sat there under his belly, a thirty dollar a week moron of a fat Babbitt bastard with a hanging gut and a girl at his side, a slut, a bitch, a whore beside him, a scummy female. Between his fat fingers he held the girl's hand. He seemed ardent in his piggish way, that fat bastard, that stinking, nauseating, thirty dollar a week moron of a rat, with his fat teeth looming in the moonlight, his big pouch squashed against the steering wheel, his dirty eyes fat and ardent with fat ideas of a fat love affair. He wasn't fooling me; he could never fool me. He might fool that girl, but not Arturo Bandini, and under no circumstances would Arturo Bandini ever consent to work for him. Some day there would be a reckoning. He might plead, with his yellow necktie dragging in the dust, he might plead with Arturo Bandini, begging the great Arturo to accept a job, and Arturo Bandini would proudly kick him in the belly and watch him writhe in the dust. He'd pay, he'd pay!

I went out to the Ford plant. And why not? Ford needs

men. Bandini at the Ford Motor Company. A week in one department, three weeks in another, a month in another, six months in another. Two years, and I would be director in chief of the Western Division.

The pavement wound through white sand, a new road heavy with monoxide gas. In the sand were brown weeds and grasshoppers. Bits of sea shell sparkled through the weeds. It was man-made land, flat and in disorder, shacks unpainted, piles of lumber, piles of tin cans, oil derricks and hot dog stands, fruit stands and old men on all sides of the road selling popcorn. Overhead the heavy telephone wires gave off a humming sound whenever there was a lull in the traffic noise. Out of the muddy channel bed came the rich stench of oil and scum and strange cargo.

I walked along the road with others. They flagged rides with their thumbs. They were beggars with jerking thumbs and pitiful smiles, begging crumbs-on-wheels. No pride. But not I — not Arturo Bandini, with his mighty legs. Not for him this mooching. Let them pass me by! Let them go ninety miles an hour and fill my nose with their exhausts. Some day it would all be different. You will pay for this, all of you, every driver along this road. I will not ride in your automobiles even if you get out and plead with me, and offer me the car to keep as my own, free and without further obligation. I will die on the road first. But my time will come, and then you will see my name in the sky. Then you shall see, every one of you! I am not waving like the others, with a crooked thumb, so don't stop. Never! But you'll pay, nevertheless.

They wouldn't give me a ride. He killed crabs, that fellow up there ahead. Why give him a ride? He loves paper ladies in clothes closets. Think of it! So don't give him a ride, that Frankenstein, that toad in the road, that black spider, snake, dog, rat, fool, monster, idiot. They wouldn't give me a ride; all right — so what! And see if I care! To hell with all of you! It suits me fine. I love to walk on these God-given legs, and by God I'll walk. Like Nietzsche. Like Kant. Immanuel Kant. What do you know about Immanuel Kant? You fools in your V-8's and Chevrolets!

When I got to the plant I stood among the others. They moved about in a thick clot before a green platform. The tight faces, the cold faces. Then a man came out. No work today, fellows. And yet there was a job or two, if you could paint, if you knew about transmissions, if you had experience, if you had worked in the Detroit plant.

But there was no work for Arturo Bandini. I saw it at a glance, and so I wouldn't let them refuse me. I was amused. This spectacle, this scene of men before a platform amused me. I'm here for a special reason, sir: a confidential mission, if I may say so, merely checking conditions for my report. The president of the United States of America sent me. Franklin Delano Roosevelt, he sent me. Frank and I—we're like that! Let me know the state of things on the Pacific Coast, Arturo; send me firsthand facts and figures; let me know in your own words what the masses are thinking out there.

And so I was a spectator. Life is a stage. Here is drama, Franklin old Kid, old Pal, old Sock; here is stark drama in the hearts of men. I'll notify the White House immediately. A telegram in code for Franklin. Frank: unrest on the Pacific Coast. Advise send twenty thousand men and guns. Population in terror. Perilous situation. Ford plant in ruins. Shall take charge personally. My word is law here. Your old buddy, Arturo.

There was an old man leaning against the wall. His nose was running clear to the tip of his chin, but he was blissful and didn't know it. It amused me. Very amusing, this old man. I'll have to make a note of this for Franklin; he loves anecdotes. Dear Frank: you'd have died if you'd have seen this old man! How Franklin will love this, chuckling as he repeats it to members of his cabinet. Say boys, did you hear the latest from my pal Arturo out on the Pacific Coast? I strolled up and down, a student of mankind, a philosopher, past the old man with the riotous nose. The philosopher out of the West contemplates the human scene.

The old man smiled his way and I smiled mine. I looked at him and he looked at me. Smile. Evidently he didn't know who I was. No doubt he confused me with the rest of the herd. Very amusing this, great sport to travel incognito. Two philosophers smiling wistfully at one another over the fate of man. He was genuinely amused, his old nose running, his blue eyes twinkling with quiet laughter. He wore blue overalls that covered him completely. Around his waist was a belt that had no purpose whatever, a useless appendage, merely a belt supporting nothing, not even his belly, for he was thin. Possibly a whim of his, something to make him laugh when he dressed in the morning.

His face beamed with a larger smile, inviting me to come forward and deliver an opinion if I liked; we were kindred souls, he and I, and no doubt he saw through my disguise and recognized a person of depth and importance, one who stood out from the herd.

"Not much today," I said. "The situation, as I see it, grows more acute daily."

He shook his head with delight, his old nose running blissfully, a Plato with a cold. A very old man, maybe eighty, with false teeth, skin like old shoes, a meaningless belt and a philosophic smile. The dark mass of men moved around us.

"Sheep!" I said. "Alas, they are sheep! Victims of Comstockery and the American system, bastard slaves of the Robber Barons. Slaves, I tell you! I wouldn't take a job at this plant if it was offered me on a golden platter! Work for this system and lose your soul. No thanks. And what does it profit a man if he gain the whole world and lose his own soul?"

He nodded, smiled, agreed, nodded for more. I warmed up. My favorite subject. Labor conditions in the machine age, a topic for a future work.

"Sheep, I tell you! A lot of gutless sheep!"

His eyes brightened. He brought out a pipe and lit it. The pipe stunk. When he took it from his mouth the goo from his nose strung after it. He wiped it off with his thumb and wiped his thumb against his leg. He didn't bother to wipe his nose. No time for that when Bandini speaks.

"It amuses me," I said. "The spectacle is priceless. Sheep getting their souls sheared. A Rabelaisian spectacle. I have to laugh." And I laughed until there wasn't anymore. He did too, slapping his thighs and shrieking to a high note until his eyes were filled with tears. Here was a man after my own heart, a man of universal humors, no doubt a well-read man despite his overalls and useless belt. From his pocket he took a pad and pencil and wrote on the pad. Now I knew: he was a writer too, of course! The secret was out. He finished writing and handed me the note.

It read: Please write it down. I am stone deaf.

No, there was no work for Arturo Bandini. I left feeling better, glad of it. I walked back wishing I had an aeroplane, a million dollars, wishing the sea shells were diamonds. I will go to the park. I am not yet a sheep. Read Nietzsche. Be a super-man. *Thus Spake Zarathustra.* Oh that Nietzsche! Don't be a sheep, Bandini. Preserve the sanctity of your mind. Go to the park and read the master under the eucalyptus trees.

SEVEN

One morning I awoke with an idea. A fine idea, big as a house. My greatest idea ever, a masterpiece. I would find a job as a night clerk in a hotel — that was the idea. This would give me a chance to read and work at the same time. I leaped out of bed, swallowed breakfast and took the stairs six at a time. On the sidewalk I stood a moment and mulled over my idea. The sun scorched the street, burning my eyes to wakefulness.

46

Strange. Now I was wide awake and the idea didn't seem so good, one of those which comes in half-sleep. A dream, a mere dream, a triviality. I couldn't get a job as a night clerk in this harbor town for the simple reason that no hotel in this harbor town used night clerks. A mathematical deduction — simple enough. I went back up the stairs to the apartment and sat down.

"Why did you run like that?" my mother asked.

"To get exercise. For my legs."

The days came with fog. The nights were nights and nothing else. The days didn't change from one to the other, the golden sun blasting away and then dying out. I was always alone. It was hard to remember such monotony. The days would not move. They stood like grey stones. Time passed slowly. Two months crawled by.

It was always the park. I read a hundred books. There was Nietzsche and Schopenhauer and Kant and Spengler and Strachey and others. Oh Spengler! What a book! What weight! Like the Los Angeles Telephone Directory. Day after day I read it, never understanding it, never caring either, but reading it because I liked one growling word after another marching across pages with somber mysterious rumblings. And Schopenhauer! What a writer! For days I read him and read him, remembering a bit here and a bit there. And such things about women! I agreed. Exactly my own feelings on the matter. Ah man, what a writer!

Once I was reading in the park. I lay on the lawn. There were little black ants among the blades of grass. They looked at me, crawling over the pages, some wondering what I was doing, others not interested and passing by. They crawled up my leg, baffled in a jungle of brown hairs, and I lifted my trousers and killed them with my thumb. They did their best to escape, diving frantically in and out of the brambles, sometimes pausing as if to trick me by their immobility, but never, for all their trickery, did they escape the menace of my thumb. What stupid ants! Bourgeois ants! That they should try to dupe one whose mind lived on the meat of Spengler and Schopenhauer and the great ones! It was their doom – the Decline of Ant Civilization. And so I read and killed ants.

It was a book called *Jews Without Money*. What a book that was! What a mother in that book! I looked from the woman on the pages and there before me on the lawn in crazy old shoes was a woman with a basket in her arms.

She was a hunchback with a sweet smile. She smiled sweetly at anything; she couldn't help it; the trees, me, the grass, anything. The basket pulled her down, dragging her toward the ground. She was such a tiny woman, with a hurt face, as if slapped forever. She wore a funny old hat, an absurd hat, a maddening hat, a hat to make me cry, a hat with faded red berries on the brim. And there she was, smiling at everything, struggling across the carpet with a heavy basket containing Lord knew what, wearing a plumed hat with red berries.

I got up. It was so mysterious. There I was, like magic, standing up, my two feet on the ground, my eyes drenched.

I said, "Let me help."

She smiled again and gave me the basket. We began to walk. She led the way. Beyond the trees it was stifling. And she smiled. It was so sweet it nearly tore my head off. She talked, she told me things I never remembered. It didn't matter. In a dream she held me, in a dream I followed under the blinding sun. For blocks we went forward. I hoped it would never end. Always she talked in a low voice made of human music. What words! What she said! I remembered nothing. I was only happy. But in my heart I was dying. It should have been so. We stepped from so many curbs, I wondered why she did not sit upon one and hold my head while I drifted away. It was the chance that never came again.

That old woman with the bent back! Old woman, I feel so joyfully your pain. Ask me a favor, you old woman you! Anything. To die is easy. Make it that. To cry is easy, lift your skirt and let me cry and let my tears wash your feet to let you know I know what life has been for you, because my back is bent too, but my heart is whole, my tears are delicious, my love is yours, to give you joy where God has failed. To die is so easy and you may have my life if you wish it, you old woman, you hurt me so, you did, I will do anything for you, to die for you, the blood of my eighteen years flowing in the gutters of Wilmington and down to the sea for you, for you that you might find such joy as is now mine and stand erect without the horror of that twist.

I left the old woman at her door.

The trees shimmered. The clouds laughed. The blue sky took me up. Where am I? Is this Wilmington, California? Haven't I been here before? A melody moved my feet. The air soared with Arturo in it, puffing him in and out and making him something and nothing. My heart laughed and laughed. Goodbye to Nietzsche and Schopenhauer and all of you, you fools, I am much greater than all of you! Through my veins ran music of blood. Would it last? It could not last. I must hurry. But where? And I ran toward home. Now I am home. I left the book in the park. To hell with it. No more books for me. I kissed my mother. I clung to her passionately. On my knees I fell at her feet to kiss her feet and cling to her ankles until it must have hurt her and amazed her that it was I.

"Forgive me," I said. "Forgive me, forgive me."

"You?" she said. "Certainly. But why?"

Ach! What a foolish woman! How did I know why? Ach! What a mother. The strangeness was gone. I got to my feet. I felt like a fool. I blushed in a bath of cold blood. What was this? I didn't know. The chair. I found it at the end of the room and sat down. My hands. They were in the way; stupid hands! Damned hands! I did something with them, got them out of the way somewhere. My breath. It hissed for horror and fear of something. My heart. It no longer tore at my chest, but dwindled,

49

crawling deep into the darkness within me. My mother. She watched me in a panic, afraid to speak, thinking me mad.

"What is it? Arturo! What's the matter?"

"None of your business."

"Shall I get a doctor?"

"Never."

"You act so strange. Are you hurt?"

"Don't talk to me. I'm thinking."

"But what is it?"

"You wouldn't know. You're a woman."

EIGHT

The days went on. A week passed. Miss Hopkins was in the library every afternoon, floating on white legs in the folds of her loose dresses in an atmosphere of books and cool thoughts. I watched. I was like a hawk. Nothing she did escaped me.

Then came a great day. What a day that was!

I was watching her from the shadows of the dark shelves. She held a book, standing behind her desk like a soldier, shoulders back, reading the book, her face so serious and so soft, her grey eyes following the beaten path of line under line. My eyes — they were so eager and so hungry they startled her. With a suddenness she looked up and her face was white with the shock of something dreadful near her. I saw her wet her lips, and then I turned away. In a while I looked again. It was like magic. Again she twitched, glanced around uneasily, put her long fingers to her throat, sighed, and commenced to read. A few moments, and once more I looked. She still held that book. But what was that book? I didn't know, but I must have it for my eyes to follow the path her eyes had followed before me.

Outside it was the evening, the sun spangling the floor in gold. With white legs as silent as ghosts she crossed the library to the windows and raised the shades. In her right hand swung that book, brushing against her dress as she walked, in her very hands, the immortal white hands of Miss Hopkins, pressed against the warm white softness of her clinging fingers.

What a book! I've got to have that book! Lord, I wanted it, to hold it, to kiss it, to crush it to my chest, that book fresh from her fingers, the very imprint of her warm fingers still upon it perhaps. Who knows? Perhaps she perspires through her fingers as she reads it. Wonderful! Then her imprint is surely upon it. I must have it. I will wait forever for it. And so I waited until seven o'clock, seeing how she held the book, the exact position of her wonderful fingers that were so slim and white, just off the back binding, no more than an inch from the bottom, the perfume of her perhaps entering those very pages and perfuming them for me.

Until at last she was finished with it. She carried it to the shelves and slipped it into a slot marked biography. I ambled by, seeking a book to read, something to stimulate my mind, something in the line of biography today, the life of some great figure, to inspire me, to make my life sublime.

Ha, there it was! The most beautiful book I ever saw, larger than the others on that shelf, a book among books, the very queen of biography, the princess of literature—that book with the blue binding. *Catherine of Aragon.* So that was it! A queen reads of another queen—most natural. And her grey eyes had followed the path of those lines—then so would mine.

I must have it—but not today. Tomorrow I will come, tomorrow. Then the other librarian, that fat and ugly one, will be on duty. Then it shall be mine, all mine. And so, until the next day, I hid the book behind others so no one could take it away while I was gone.

I was there early next day—at nine o'clock to the second. Catherine of Aragon: wonderful woman, the Queen of England, the bedmate of Henry VIII—that much I knew already.

Undoubtedly Miss Hopkins had read of the intimacy of Catherine and Henry in this book. Those sections dealing with love – did they delight Miss Hopkins? Did shivers run down her back? Did she breathe hard, her bosom swelling, and a mysterious tingling enter her fingers? Yes, and who knew? Perhaps she even screamed for joy and felt a mysterious stirring somewhere within her, the call of womanhood. Yes indeed, no doubt about it at all. And wonderful too. A thing of great beauty, a thought to ponder over. And so I got the book, and there it was, in my own two hands. To think of it! Yesterday she had held it with her fingers warm and close, and today it was mine. Marvelous. An act of destiny. A miracle of succession. When we married I would tell Miss Hopkins about it. We would be lying stark naked in bed and I would kiss her on the lips and laugh softly and triumphantly and tell her that the real beginning of my love was on a day I saw her reading a certain book. And I would laugh again, my white teeth flashing, my dark romantic eyes aglow as I told her at last the real truth of my provocative and eternal love. Then she would crush herself to me, her beautiful white breasts full against me, and tears would stream down her face as I carried her away on wave after wave of ecstasy. What a day!

I held the book close to my eyes, searching for some trace of white fingers no more than an inch from the bottom. There were finger-prints all right. No matter if they belonged to so many others, they nevertheless belonged to Miss Hopkins alone. Walking toward the park I kissed them, and I kissed them so much that finally they were gone altogether, and only a blue wet spot remained on the book, while on my mouth I tasted the sweet taste of blue dye. In the park I found my favorite spot and began to read.

Near the bridge it was, and I made a shrine from twigs and blades of grass. It was the throne of Miss Hopkins. Ah, if she but knew it! But at that moment she was at home in Los

Angeles, far away from the scene of her devotions, and not thinking of them at all.

I crawled on all fours to the place at the edge of the lily pond where roamed bugs and crickets, and I caught a cricket. A black cricket, fat and well-built, with electric energy in his body. And there he lay in my hand, that cricket, and he was I, the cricket that was, he was I, Arturo Bandini, black and undeserving of the fair white princess, and I lay on my belly and watched him crawl over the places her sacred white fingers had touched, he too enjoying as he passed the sweet taste of blue dye. Then he tried to escape. With a jump he was on his way. I was forced to break his legs. There was absolutely no alternative.

I said to him, "Bandini, I am sorry. But duty compels me. The Queen wishes it – the beloved Queen."

Now he crawled painfully, in wonder at what had taken place. Oh fair white Miss Hopkins, observe! Oh queen of all the heavens and the earth. Observe! I crawl at thy feet, a mere black cricket, a scoundrel, unworthy to be called human. Here I lie with broken legs, a paltry black cricket, ready to die for thee; aye, already nearing death. Ah! Reduce me to ashes! Give me a new form! Make me a man! Snuff out my life for the glory of love everlasting and the loveliness of your white legs!

And I killed the black cricket, crushing him to death after proper farewells between the pages of *Catherine of Aragon*, his poor miserable unworthy black body crackling and popping in ecstasy and love there at that sacred little shrine of Miss Hopkins.

And behold! A miracle: out of death came life everlasting. The resurrection of life. The cricket was no more, but the power of love had found its way, and I was again myself and no longer a cricket, I was Arturo Bandini, and the elm tree yonder was Miss Hopkins, and I got to my knees and put my arms around the tree, kissing it for love everlasting, tearing the bark with my teeth and spitting it on the lawn.

I turned around and bowed to the bushes at the edge of

the pond. They applauded gloriously, swaying together, hissing their delight and satisfaction at the scene, even demanding that I carry Miss Hopkins away on my shoulders. This I refused to do, and with sly winks and suggestive movements I told them why, because the fair white queen didn't want to be carried, if you please, she wanted instead to be laid flat, and at this they all laughed and thought me the greatest lover and hero to ever visit their fair country.

"You understand, fellows. We prefer to be alone, the queen and I. There is much unfinished business between us — if you get what I mean."

Laughter, and wild applauding from the bushes.

NINE

One night my uncle dropped in. He gave my mother some money. He could only stay a moment. He said he had good news for me. I wanted to know what he meant. A job, he said. At last he had found me a job. I told him this was not good news, necessarily, because I didn't know what kind of a job he got me. To this he told me to shut up, and then he told me about the job.

He said, "Take this down and tell him I sent you."

He handed me the note he had already written.

"I talked to him today," he said. "Everything is set. Do what you're told, keep your fool mouth shut, and he'll keep you on steady."

"He ought to," I said. "Any paranoiac can do cannery work."

"We'll see about that," my uncle said.

Next morning I took the bus for the harbor. It was only seven blocks from our house, but since I was going to work I thought it best not to tire myself by walking too much. The Soyo

Fish Company bulged from the channel like a black dead whale. Steam spouted from pipes and windows.

At the front office sat a girl. This was a strange office. At a desk with no papers or pencils upon it, sat this girl. She was an ugly girl with a hooknose who wore glasses and a yellow skirt. She sat at the desk doing absolutely nothing, no telephone, not even a pencil before her.

"Hello," I said.

"That's not necessary," she said. "Who do you want?"

I told her I wanted to see a man named Shorty Naylor. I had a note for him. She wanted to know what the note was about. I gave it to her and she read it. "For pity's sakes," she said. Then she told me to wait a minute. She got up and went out. At the door she turned around and said, "Don't touch anything, please." I told her I wouldn't. But when I looked about I saw nothing to touch. In the corner on the floor was a full tin of sardines, unopened. It was all I could see in the room, except for the desk and chair. She's a maniac, I thought; she's dementia praecox.

As I waited I could feel something. A stench in the air all at once began to suck at my stomach. It pulled my stomach toward my throat. Leaning back, I felt the sucking. I began to feel afraid. It was like an elevator going down too fast.

Then the girl returned. She was alone. But no — she wasn't alone. Behind her, and unseen until she stepped out of the way, was a little man. This man was Shorty Naylor. He was much smaller than I was. He was very thin. His collarbones stuck out. He had no teeth worth mentioning in his mouth, only one or two which were worse than nothing. His eyes were like aged oysters on a sheet of newspaper. Tobacco juice caked the corners of his mouth like dry chocolate. His was the look of a rat in waiting. It seemed he had never been out in the sun, his face was so grey. He didn't look at my face but at my belly. I wondered what he saw there. I looked down. There was nothing, merely a belly, no larger than ever and not worth observation. He took the note from my hands. His fingernails were gnawed to stumps. He read the note bitterly, much annoyed, crushed it, and stuck it in his pocket.

"The pay is twenty-five cents an hour," he said.

"That's preposterous and nefarious."

"Anyway, that's what it is."

The girl was sitting on the desk watching us. She was smiling at Shorty. It was as if there was some joke. I couldn't see anything funny. I lifted my shoulders. Shorty was ready to go back through the door from which he had come.

"The pay is of little consequence," I said. "The facts in the case make the matter different. I am a writer. I interpret the American scene. My purpose here is not the gathering of money but the gathering of material for my forthcoming book on California fisheries. My income of course is much larger than what I shall make here. But that, I suppose, is a matter of no great consequence at the moment, none at all."

"No," he said. "The pay is twenty-five cents an hour."

"It doesn't matter. Five cents or twenty-five. Under the circumstances, it doesn't matter in the least. Not at all. I am, as I say, a writer. I interpret the American scene. I am here to gather material for my new work."

"Oh for Christ's sake!" the girl said, turning her back. "For the love of God get him out of here."

"I don't like Americans in my crew," Shorty said. "They don't work hard like the other boys."

"Ah," I said. "That's where you're wrong, sir. My patriotism is universal. I swear allegiance to no flag."

"Jesus," the girl said.

But she was ugly. Nothing she could possibly say would ever disturb me. She was too ugly.

"Americans can's stand the pace," Shorty said. "Soon as they get a bellyful they quit."

"Interesting, Mr. Naylor." I folded my arms and settled back on my heels. "Extremely interesting what you say there. A fascinating sociological aspect of the canning situation. My book will go into that with great detail and footnotes. I'll quote you there. Yes, indeed."

The girl said something unprintable. Shorty scraped a bit of pocket sediment from a plug of tobacco and bit off a hunk. It was a large bite, filling his mouth. He was scarcely listening to me, I could tell by the scrupulous way he chewed the tobacco. The girl had seated herself at the desk, her hands folded before her. We both turned and looked at one another. She put her fingers to her nose and pressed them. But the gesture didn't disturb me. She was far too ugly.

"Do you want the job?" Shorty said.

"Yes, under the circumstances. Yes."

"Remember: the work is hard, and don't expect no favors from me either. If it wasn't for your uncle I wouldn't hire you, but that's as far as it goes. I don't like you Americans. You're lazy. When you get tired you quit. You fool around too much."

"I agree with you perfectly, Mr. Naylor. I agree with you thoroughly. Laziness, if I may be permitted to make an aside, laziness is the outstanding characteristic of the American scene. Do you follow me?"

"You don't have to call me Mister. Call me Shorty. That's my name."

"Certainly, sir! But by all means, certainly! And Shorty, I would say, is a most colorful sobriquet — a typical Americanism. We writers are constantly coming upon it."

This failed to please him or impress him. His lip curled. At the desk the girl was mumbling. "Don't call me sir, neither," Shorty said. "I don't like none of that high-toned crap."

"Take him out of here," the girl said.

But I was not in the least disturbed by the remarks from one so ugly. It amused me. What an ugly face she had! It was too amusing for words. I laughed and patted Shorty on the back. I was short, but I towered over this small man. I felt great—like a giant.

"Very amusing, Shorty. I love your native sense of humor. Very amusing. Very amusing indeed." And I laughed again. "Very amusing. Ho, ho, ho. How very amusing."

"I don't see nothing funny," he said.

"But it is! If you follow me."

"The hell with it. You follow me."

"Oh, I follow you, all right. I follow."

"No," he said. "I mean, you follow me now. I'll put you in the labeling crew."

As we walked through the back door the girl turned to watch us go. "And stay out of here!" she said. But I paid no attention at all. She was far too ugly.

We were inside the cannery works. The corrugated iron building was like a dark hot dungeon. Water dripped from the girders. Lumps of brown and white steam hung bloated in the air. The green floor was slippery from fish oil. We walked across a long room where Mexican and Japanese women stood before tables gutting mackerel with fish knives. The women were wrapped in heavy oil-skins, their feet cased in rubber boots ankle-deep in fish guts.

The stench was too much. All at once I was sick like the sickness from hot water and mustard. Another ten steps across the room and I felt it coming up, my breakfast, and I bent over to let it go. My insides rushed out in a chunk. Shorty laughed. He pounded my back and roared. Then the others started. The boss was laughing at something, and so did they. I hated it. The women looked up from their work to see, and they laughed. What fun! On company time, too! See the boss laughing! Something must be taking place. Then we will laugh too. Work was stopped in the cutting room. Everybody was laughing. Everybody but Arturo Bandini.

Arturo Bandini was not laughing. He was puking his guts out on the floor. I hated every one of them, and I vowed revenge, staggering away, wanting to be out of sight somewhere. Shorty took me by the arm and led me toward another door. I leaned against the wall and got my breath. But the stench charged again. The walls spun, the women laughed, and Shorty laughed, and Arturo Bandini the great writer was heaving again. How he heaved! The women would go home tonight and talk about it at their houses. That new fellow! You should have seen him! And I hated them and even stopped heaving for a moment to pause and delight over the fact that this was the greatest hatred of all my life.

"Feel better?" Shorty said.

"Of course," I said. "It was nothing. The idiosyncrasies of an artistic stomach. A mere nothing. Something I ate, if you will."

"That's right!"

We walked into the room beyond. The women were still laughing on company time. At the door Shorty Naylor turned around and put a scowl on his face. Nothing more. He merely scowled. All the women stopped laughing. The show was over. They went back to work.

Now we were in the room where the cans were labeled. The crew was made up of Mexican and Filipino boys. They fed the machines from flat conveyor lines. Twenty or more of them, my age and more, all of them pausing to see who I was and realizing that a new man was about to go to work.

"You stand and watch," Shorty said. "Pitch in when you see how they do it."

"It looks very simple," I said. "I'm ready right now."

"No. Wait a few minutes."

And he left.

I stood watching. This was very simple. But my stomach would have nothing to do with it. In a moment I was letting go

59

again. Again the laughter. But these boys weren't like the women. They really thought it was funny to see Arturo Bandini having such a time of it.

That first morning had no beginning and no end. Between vomitings I stood at the can dump and convulsed. And I told them who I was. Arturo Bandini, the writer. Haven't you heard of me? You will! Don't worry. You will! My book on California fisheries. It is going to be the standard work on the subject. I spoke fast, between vomitings.

"I'm not here permanently. I'm gathering material for a book on California Fisheries. I'm Bandini, the writer. This isn't essential, this job. I may give my wages to charity: the Salvation Army."

And I heaved again. Now there was nothing in my stomach except that which never came out. I bent over and choked, a famous writer with my arms around my waist, squirming and choking. But nothing would come. Somebody stopped laughing long enough to yell that I should drink water. Hey writer! Dreenk water! So I found a hydrant and drank water. It came out in a stream while I raced for the door. And they laughed. Oh that writer! What a writer he was! See him write!

"You get over it," they laughed.

"Go home," they said. "Go write book. You writer. You too good for feesh cannery. Go home and write book about puke."

Shrieks of laughter.

I walked outside and stretched out on a pile of fish nets hot in the sun between two buildings away from the main road that skirted the channel. Over the hum from the machinery I could hear them laughing. I didn't care, not all. I felt like sleeping. But the fish nets were bad, rich with the smell of mackerel and salt. In a moment the flies discovered me. That made it worse. Soon all the flies in Los Angeles Harbor had got news of me. I crawled off the nets to a patch of sand. It was wonderful. I stretched my arms and let my fingers find cool spots in the sand. Nothing ever felt so good. Even little particles of sand my breath blew were sweet in my nose and mouth. A tiny sandbug stopped on a hill to investigate the commotion. Ordinarily I would have killed him without hesitating. He looked into my eyes, paused, and came forward. He began to climb my chin.

"Go ahead," I said. "I don't mind. You can go into my mouth if you want to."

He passed my chin and I felt him tickle my lips. I had to look at him cross-eyed to see him.

"Come ahead," I said. "I'm not going to hurt you. This is a holiday."

He climbed toward my nostrils. Then I went to sleep.

A whistle woke me up. It was twelve o'clock, noon. The workers filed out of the buildings, Mexicans, Filipinos, and Japanese. The Japanese were too busy to look anywhere other than straight ahead. They hurried by. But the Mexicans and Filipinos saw me stretched out, and they laughed again, for there he was, that great writer, all flattened out like a drunkard.

It had got all over the cannery by this time that a great personality was in their midst, none other than that immortal Arturo Bandini, the writer, and there he lay, no doubt composing something for the ages, this great writer who made fish his specialty, who worked for a mere twenty-five cents an hour because he was so democratic, that great writer. So great he was indeed, that — well, there he sprawled, flat on his belly in the sun, puking his guts out, too sick to stand the smell he was going to write a book about. A book on California fisheries! Oh, what a writer! A book on California puke! Oh, what a writer he is!

Laughter.

Thirty minutes passed. The whistle blew again. They streamed back from the lunch counters. I rolled over and saw them pass, blurred in shape, a bilious dream. The bright sun was sickening. I buried my face in my arm. They were still enjoying it, but not so much as before, because the great writer was beginning to bore them. Lifting my head I saw them out of sticky eyes as the stream moved by. They were munching apples, licking ice-cream bars, eating chocolate covered candy from noisy packages. The nausea returned. My stomach grumbled, kicked, rebelled.

Hey writer! Hey writer! Hey writer!

I heard them gather around me, the laughter and the cackling. Hey writer! The voices were shattered echoes. The dust from their feet rolled in lazy clouds. Then louder than ever a mouth against my ear, and a shout. Heeey writer! Arms grabbed me, lifted me up and turned me over. Before it happened I knew what they were going to do. This was their idea of a really funny episode. They were going to stick a fish down my waist. I knew it without even seeing the fish. I lay on my back. The mid-day sun smeared my face. I felt fingers at my shirt and the rip of cloth. Of course! Just as I thought! They were going to stick that fish down my waist. But I never even saw the fish. I kept my eyes closed. Then something cold and clammy pressed my chest and was pushed down to my belt: that fish! The fools. I knew it a long time before they did it. I just *knew* they were going to do that. But I didn't feel like caring. One fish more or less didn't matter now.

TEN

Time passed. Maybe a half hour. I reached into my shirt and felt the fish against my skin. I ran my fingers along the surface, feeling his fins and tail. Now I felt better. I pulled the fish out, held him up, and looked at him. A mackerel, a foot long. I held my breath so I would not smell him. Then I put him in my mouth and bit off his head. I was sorry he was already dead. I threw him aside and got to my feet. There were some big flies making a feast of my face and the wet spot on my shirt where the fish had lain. A bold fly landed on my arm and stubbornly refused to move, even though I warned him by shaking my arm. This made me insanely angry with him. I slapped him, killing him on my arm. But I was still so furious with him that I put him in my mouth and chewed him to bits and spat him out. Then I got the fish again, placed him on a level spot in the sand, and jumped on him until he burst open. The whiteness of my face was a thing I could feel, like plaster. Every time I moved a hundred flies dispersed. The flies were such idiotic fools. I stood still, killing them, but even the dead among them taught the living nothing. They still insisted on annoying me. For some time I stood patiently and quietly, scarcely breathing, watching the flies move into a position where I could kill them.

The nausea was past. I had forgotten that part of it. What I hated was the laughter, the flies, and the dead fish. Again I wished that fish had been alive. He would have been taught a lesson not soon forgotten. I didn't know what would happen next. I would get even with them. Bandini never forgets. He will find a way. You shall pay for this — all of you.

Just across the way was the lavatory. I started for it. Two impudent flies followed me. I stopped dead in my tracks, fuming, still as a statue, waiting for the flies to land. At last I got one of them. The other escaped. I pulled off the fly's wings and dropped him to the ground. He crawled about in the dirt, darting like a fish, thinking he would escape me in that fashion. It was preposterous. For a while I let him do so to his heart's desire. Then I jumped on him with both feet and crushed him into the ground. I built a mound over the spot, and spat upon it.

In the lavatory I swayed back and forth like a rocking chair, standing and wondering what to do next, trying to get hold of myself. There were too many cannery workers for a fight. I had already settled with the flies and the dead fish, but not the cannery workers. You couldn't kill cannery workers the way you killed flies. It had to be something else, some way of fighting

63

without fists. I washed my face in cold water and thought about it.

In walked a dark Filipino. He was one of the boys from the labeling crew. He stood at the trough along the wall, fighting buttons impatiently and frowning. Then he solved the buttons and was relieved, smiling all the time and shivering a bit for ease. Now he felt a lot better. I leaned over the sink at the opposite wall and let the water run through my hair and over my neck. The Filipino turned around and began again with the buttons. He lit a cigarette and stood against the wall watching me. He did it on purpose, watching me in such a way that I would know he was watching me and nothing else. But I wasn't afraid of him. I was never afraid of him. Nobody in California was ever afraid of a Filipino. He smiled to let me know he didn't think much of me either, or of my weak stomach. I straightened up and let the water drip from my face. It fell to my dusty shoes, making bright dots on them. The Filipino thought less and less of me. Now he was no longer smiling but sneering.

"How you feel?" he said.

"What business is it of yours?"

He was slender and over medium height. I wasn't as large as he, but I was perhaps as heavy. I leered at him from head to foot. I even stuck out my chin and pulled back my lower lip to denote the zenith of contempt. He leered back, but in a different way, not with his chin out. He was not in the least afraid of me. If something didn't happen to interrupt it, his courage would soon be so great that he would insult me.

His skin was a nut brown. I noticed it because his teeth were so white. They were brilliant teeth, like a row of pearls. When I saw how dark he was I suddenly knew what to say to him. I could say it to all of them. It would hurt them every time. I knew because a thing like that had hurt me. In grade school the kids used to hurt me by calling me Wop and Dago. It had hurt every time. It was a miserable feeling. It used to make me feel so pitiful, so unworthy. And I knew it would hurt the Filipino too. It was so easy to do that all at once I was laughing quietly at him, and over me came a cool, confident feeling, at ease with everything. I couldn't fail. I walked close to him and put my face near his, smiling the way he smiled. He could tell something was coming. Immediately his expression changed. He was waiting for it — whatever it was.

"Give me a cigarette," I said. "You nigger."

That hit him. Ah, but he felt that baby. Instantly there was a change, a shift of feelings, the movement from offense to defense. The smile hardened on his face and his face was frozen: he wanted to keep smiling but he couldn't. Now he hated me. His eyes sharpened. It was a wonderful feeling. He could escape his own squirming. It was open to the whole world. It had been that way with me too. Once in a drug store a girl had called me a Dago. I was only ten years old, but all at once I hated that girl the way the Filipino hated me. I had offered to buy the girl an ice-cream cone. She wouldn't take it, saying, my mother told me not to have anything to do with you because you're a Dago. And I decided I would do it to the Filipino again.

"You're not a nigger at all," I said. "You're a damn Filipino, which is worse."

But now his face was neither brown nor black. It was purple.

"A yellow Filipino. A damn oriental foreigner! Doesn't it make you uncomfortable to be around white people?"

He didn't want to talk about it. He shook his head quickly in denial.

"Christ," I said. "Look at your face! You're as yellow as a canary."

And I laughed. I bent over and shrieked. I pointed my finger at his face and shrieked until I could no longer pretend that the laughter was genuine. His face was tight as ice with pain and humiliation, his mouth lodged in helplessness, like a mouth stuck on a stick, uncertain and aching.

JOHN FANTE

"Boy!" I said. "You came close to fooling me. All the time I thought you were a nigger. And here you turn out to be yellow."

Then he softened. His cloggy face loosened. He made a weak smile of jelly and water. Colors moved across his face. He looked down at his shirt front and brushed away a streak of cigarette ash. Then he raised his eyes.

"You feel better now?" he asked.

I said, "What do you care? You're a Filipino. You Filipinos don't get sick because you're used to this slop. I'm a writer, man! An American writer, man! Not a Filipino writer. I wasn't born in the Philippine Islands. I was born right here in the good old U.S.A. under the stars and stripes."

Shrugging, he couldn't make much sense out of what I said. "Me no writer," he smiled. "No no no. I born in Honolulu."

"That's just it!" I said. "That's the difference. I write books, man! What do you Orientals expect? I write books in the mother tongue, the English language. I'm no slimy Oriental."

For the third time he said, "You feel better now?"

"What do you expect!" I said. "I write books, you fool! Tomes! I wasn't born in Honolulu. I was born right here in good old Southern California."

He flipped his cigarette across the room to the trough. It hit the wall with sparks flying and then landed not in the trough but on the floor.

"I go now," he said. "You come pretty soon, no?"

"Give me a cigarette."

"No got none."

He moved toward the door.

"No more. Last one."

But there was a pack bulging from his shirt pocket.

"You yellow Filipino liar," I said. "What're those?"

He grinned and took out the package, offering me one. They were a cheaper brand, a ten cent cigarette. I pushed them away.

66

"Filipino cigarettes. No thanks. Not for me."

That was all right with him.

"I see you later," he said.

"Not if I see you first."

He went away. I heard his feet moving away on the gravel path. I was alone. His discarded cigarette butt lay on the floor. I tore away the wet and smoked it to my fingertips. When I could no longer hold it I dropped it to the floor and crushed it with my heel. That for you! And I ground it to a brown spot. It had had a different taste than ordinary cigarettes; somehow it tasted more like a Filipino than like tobacco.

It was cool in the room with so much water always running in the trough. I went to the window and relaxed, with my face in my hands, watching the afternoon sun cut a bar of silver through the dust. There was a wire net across the window, with holes an inch square. I thought about the Black Hole of Calcutta. The English soldiers had died in a room no larger than this. But this was an altogether different kind of room. There was more ventilation in it. All of this thinking was only of the moment. It had nothing to do with anything. All little rooms reminded me of the Black Hole of Calcutta, and that made me think of Macaulay. So now I stood at the window thinking of Macaulay. The stench was endurable now; it was unpleasant, but I had got used to it. I was hungry without an appetite, but I couldn't think about food. I still had to face again the boys in the labeling crew. I looked about for another cigarette butt, but could not find any. Then I walked out.

Three Mexican girls walked down the path toward the washroom. They had just come out of the cutting room. I rounded the corner of the building, which was bashed in, as if a truck had smashed it. The girls saw me and I saw them. They were right in the middle of the path. They put their heads together. They were saying that here was that writer again, or something like that.

I drew nearer. The girl in boots nodded toward me. When I came closer they all smiled. I smiled back. We were ten feet apart. I could feel the girl in boots. It was because of her high breasts, they excited me so, all of a sudden, but it was nothing, only a flash, something to think about later on. I stopped in the middle of the path. I spread my legs and barred the path. Frightened, they slowed down; the writer was up to something. The girl in the house cap spoke heatedly to the girl in boots.

"Let's go back," the girl in boots said.

I could feel her again, and I made up my mind to give her a great deal of thought some other time. Then the third girl, the girl who smoked a cigarette, spoke in quick sharp Spanish. Now the three of them tipped their heads arrogantly and started toward me. I addressed the girl in boots. She was the prettiest. The others were not worth speaking to, being much inferior in looks to the girl in boots.

"Well well well," I said. "Greetings to the three pretty Filipino girls!"

They weren't Filipinos at all, not in the least, and I knew it and they knew I knew it. They breezed by snootily, their noses in the air. I had to get out of their way or be bumped off the path. The girl in boots had white arms that curved as easily as a milk bottle. But near her I saw that she was ugly, with tiny purple pimples and a smear of powder on her throat. It was a disappointment. She turned around and made a face at me; she stuck out her pink tongue and puckered her nose.

This was a surprise, and I was glad, because I was expert at making horrible faces. I pulled my eyelids down, showed my teeth, and screwed up my cheeks. The face I made was much more horrible than hers. She walked backward, facing me, her pink tongue out, making all kinds of faces, but all of them variations of the stick-out-your-tongue kind. Each of mine were better than hers. The two other girls walked straight ahead. The boots of the girl-in-boots were too big for her feet; they slushed in the dust as she walked backward. I liked the way the hem of her dress flapped over her legs, the dust coming aburst like a big grey flower all around her.

"That's no way for a Filipino girl to act!" I said.

It infuriated her.

"We're *not* Filipinos!" she screamed. "*You're* the Filipino! Filipino! Filipino!"

Now the other girls turned around. They pitched into the refrain. All three of them walked backward, arm in arm, and shrilled in sing-song.

"Filipino! Filipino! Filipino!"

They made more monkey faces and thumbed their noses at me. The distance between us widened. I raised my arm for them to keep still a minute. They had done most of the talking and shouting. I had scarcely said anything yet. But they kept up the sing-song. I waved my arms and put my finger to my lips for quiet. Finally they consented to stop and listen. At last I had the floor. They were so far away, and there was so much noise coming from the buildings that I had to cup my hands and yell.

"I beg your pardon!" I yelled. "Excuse me for making a mistake! I'm awfully sorry! I thought you were Filipinos. But you're not. You're a lot worse! You're Mexicans! You're Greasers! You're Spick sluts! Spick sluts! Spick sluts!"

I was a hundred feet away, but I could feel their sudden apathy. It came down upon each of them, jarring them, hurting them silently, each ashamed to admit the pain to the other, yet each giving away the secret hurt by keeping so still. That had happened to me too. Once I licked a boy in a fight. I felt fine until I began to walk away. He got up and ran toward home, shouting that I was a Dago. There were other boys standing around. The shouts of the retreating boy made me feel as the Mexican girls felt. Now I laughed at the Mexican girls. I lifted my mouth to the sky and laughed, not once turning to look back, but laughing so loud I knew they heard me. Then I went inside.

"Nyah nyah nyah!" I said. "Jabber jabber jabber!"
But I felt crazy for doing it. And they thought I was crazy.
They looked dumbfounded at one another and then back at me.
They didn't know I was trying to ridicule them. No, the way they
shook their heads they were convinced I was a lunatic.

But now for the young fellows in the labeling room. This
was going to be the hardest. I walked in with quick meaningful
strides, whistling all the time, and taking deep breaths to show
them the stench had no effect upon me. I even rubbed my chest
and said, ah! The boys were packed around the can dump, direct-
ing the flow of cans as they tumbled toward the greasy belt that
carried them to the machines. They were crowded shoulder to
shoulder around the box-shaped dump that measured ten feet
square. The room was as noisy as it was stinking, full of all
manner of dead fish odors. There was such noise that they didn't
notice me coming. I nudged my shoulder between two big Mexicans who were talking as they worked. I made a big fuss, squirming and prying my way through. Then they looked down and
saw me between them. It annoyed them. They couldn't understand what I was trying to do until I spread them apart with my
elbows and my arms were finally free.

I yelled, "One side, you Greasers!"

"Bah!" the largest Mexican said. "Leave heem alone, Joe.
The leetle son of a beetch is crazee."

I plunged in and worked, straightening cans for their positions on the conveyor belts. They were leaving me alone for sure,
with plenty of freedom. Nobody spoke. I felt alone indeed. I felt
like a corpse, and that the only reason I was there was because
they could do nothing about it.

The afternoon waned.

I stopped work only twice. Once to get a drink of water,
and the other time to write something in my little notebook. Every
one of them stopped work to watch me when I stepped off the
platform to make the notation in my book. This was to prove

70

to them without a doubt that after all I wasn't fooling, that I was a real writer among them, the real thing, and not a fake. I looked scrutinizingly at every face and scratched my ear with a pencil. Then for a second I gazed off into space. Finally I snapped my fingers to show that the thought had come through with flying colors. I put the notebook on my knee and wrote.

I wrote: Friends, Romans, and countrymen! All of Gaul is divided into three parts. Thou goest to woman? Do not forget thy whip. Time and tide wait for no man. Under the spreading chestnut tree the village smithy stands. Then I stopped to sign it with a flourish. Arturo G. Bandini. I couldn't think of anything else. With popping eyes they watched me. I made up my mind that I must think of something else. But that was all. My mind had quit functioning altogether. I could not think of another item, not even a word, not even my own name.

I put the notebook back into my pocket and took my place on the can dump. None of them said a word. Now their doubts were surely shaken. Hadn't I stopped work to do a bit of writing? Perhaps they had judged me too hastily. I hoped someone would ask me what I had written. Quickly I would tell him that it was nothing important, merely a notation concerning the foreign labor conditions in my regular report to the House Ways and Means Committee; nothing you'd understand, old fellow; it's too deep to explain now; some other time; perhaps at lunch some day.

Now they began talking again. Then together they laughed. But it was all Spanish to me, and I understood nothing.

The boy they called Jugo jumped out of line as I had done and pulled a notebook from his pocket too. He ran to where I had stood with my notebook. For a second I thought he must really be a writer who had observed something valuable. He took the same position I had taken. He scratched his ear the way I had scratched mine. He looked off into space the way I had done. Then he wrote. Roars of laughter.

"Me writer too!" he said. "Look!"

He held the notebook up for all to see. He had drawn a cow. The cow's face was spotted as if with freckles. This was unquestionably ridicule, because I had a face filled with freckles. Under the cow he had written "Writer." He carried the notebook around the can dump.

"Very funny," I said. "Greaser comedy."

I hated him so much it nauseated me. I hated every one of them and the clothes they wore and everything about them. We worked until six o'clock. All that afternoon Shorty Naylor did not appear. When the whistle blew the boys dropped everything and rushed from the platform. I stayed on a few minutes, picking up cans that had fallen to the floor. I hoped Shorty would return at that moment. For ten minutes I worked, but not a soul came to watch me, so I quit in disgust, throwing all the cans back on the floor.

ELEVEN

At a quarter after six I was on my way home. The sun was slipping behind the big dock warehouses and the long shadows were on the ground. What a day! What a hell of a day! I walked along talking to myself about it, discussing it. I always did that, talking aloud to myself in a heavy whisper. Usually it was fun, because I always had the right answers. But not that night. I hated the mumbling that went on inside my mouth. It was like the drone of a trapped bumblebee. The part of me which supplied answers to my questions kept saying Oh nuts! You crazy liar! You fool! You jack-ass! Why don't you tell the truth once in a while? It's your fault, so quit trying to shift the blame onto somebody else.

I crossed the schoolyard. Near the iron fence was a palm tree growing all by itself. The earth was freshly turned about the roots, a young tree I had never seen before growing in that place.

I stopped to look at it. There was a bronze plaque at the foot of the tree. It read: Planted by the children of Banning High in commemoration of Mother's Day.

I took a branch of the tree in my fingers and shook hands with it. "Hello," I said. "You weren't there, but whose fault would you say it was?"

It was a small tree, no taller than myself, and not more than a year old. It answered with a sweet plashing of thick leaves.

"The women," I said. "Do you think they had anything to do with it?"

Not a word from the tree.

"Yes. It's the fault of the women. They have enslaved my mind. They alone are responsible for what happened today."

The tree swayed slightly.

"The women have got to be annihilated. Positively annihilated. I must get them out of my mind forever. They and they alone have made me what I am today.

"Tonight the women die. This is the hour of decision. The time has come. My destiny is clear before me. It is death, death, death for the women tonight. I have spoken."

I shook hands with the tree again and crossed the street. Traveling with me was the stench of fish, a shadow that could not be seen but smelled. It followed me up the apartment steps. The moment I stepped inside the apartment the smell was everywhere, drifting straight for every corner of the apartment. Like an arrow it traveled to Mona's nostrils. She walked out of the bedroom with a nail file in her hand and a searching look in her eyes.

"Peeeew!" she said. "What *is* that?"

"It's me. The smell of honest labor. What of it?"

She put a handkerchief to her nose.

I said, "It's probably too delicate for the nostrils of a sanctified nun."

My mother was in the kitchen. She heard our voices. The

door swung open and she emerged, moving into the room. The stench attacked her. It hit her in the face like a lemon pie in the two-act comedies. She stopped dead in her tracks. A sniff and her face tightened. Then she backed up.

"Smell him!" Mona said.

"I thought I smelt *something!*" my mother said.

"It's me. The smell of honest labor. It's a man's smell. It's not for effetes and dilettantes. It's fish."

"It's disgusting," Mona said.

"Bilge," I said. "Who are you to criticize a smell? You're a nun. A female. A mere woman. You're not even a woman because you're a nun. You're only half-woman."

"Arturo," my mother said. "Let's not have any talk like that."

"A nun ought to like the smell of fish."

"Naturally. That's what I've been telling you for the last half hour."

My mother's hands rose to the ceiling, her fingers trembling. It was a gesture that always came before tears. Her voice cracked, went out of control, and the tears burst forth.

"Thank God! Oh thank God!"

"A lot he had to do with it. I got this job myself. I'm an atheist. I deny the hypothesis of God."

Mona sneered.

"How you talk! You couldn't get a job to save your life. Uncle Frank got it for you."

"That's a lie, a filthy lie. I tore up Uncle Frank's note."

"I believe that."

"I don't care what you believe. Anybody who gives credence to the Virgin Birth and the Resurrection is a plain boob whose beliefs are all under suspicion."

Silence.

"I am now a worker," I said. "I belong to the proletariat. I am a writer-worker."

Mona smiled.

"You'd smell much better if you were only a writer."

"I love this smell," I told her. "I love its every connotation and ramification; every variation and implication fascinates me. I belong to the people."

Her mouth puckered.

"Mamma, listen to him! Using words without knowing what they mean."

I could not tolerate a remark like that. It burned me to the core. She could ridicule my beliefs and persecute me for my philosophy and I would not complain. But no one could make fun of my English. I ran across the room.

"Don't insult me! I can endure a lot of your bilge and folderol, but in the name of the Jehovah you worship, don't insult me!"

I shook my fist in her face and butted her with my chest. "I can stand a lot of your imbecilities, but in the name of your monstrous Yahweh, you sanctimonious, she-nun of a God-worshipping pagan nun of a good-for-nothing scum of the earth, don't insult me! I oppose it. I oppose it emphatically!"

She tilted her chin and pushed me away with her fingertips.

"Please go away. Take a bath. You smell bad."

I swung at her, and the tips of my fingers flecked her face. She clenched her teeth and stamped the floor with both feet.

"You fool! You fool!"

My mother was always too late. She got between us.

"Here, here! What's all this about?"

I hitched up my pants and sneered at Mona.

"It's about time I had supper. That's what it's all about. As long as I'm supporting two parasitical women I guess I'm entitled to something to eat once in a while."

I peeled off my stinking shirt and threw it on a chair in the corner. Mona got it, carried it to the window, opened the window, and threw it out. Then she swung around and defied

me to do something about it. I said nothing, merely staring at
her coldly to let her know the depth of my contempt. My mother
stood dumbfounded, unable to understand what was going on;
not in a million years would she have thought to throw away
a shirt simply because it stunk. Without speaking I hurried
downstairs and around the house. The shirt hung from a fig tree
below our window. I put it on and returned to the apartment.
I stood in the exact spot I had stood before. I folded my arms
and allowed the contempt to gush from my face.

"Now," I said. "Try that again. I dare you!"

"You fool!" Mona said. "Uncle Frank's right. You're insane."

"Ho. Him! That boobus Americanus ass."

My mother was horrified. Every time I said something she
did not understand she thought it had something to do with sex
or naked women.

"Arturo! To think of it! Your own uncle!"

"Uncle or not. I positively refuse to retract the charge. He's
a boobus Americanus now and forever."

"But your own uncle! Your own flesh and blood!"

"My attitude is unchanged. The charge stands."

Supper was spread in the breakfast nook. I didn't wash
up. I was too hungry. I went in and sat down. My mother came,
bringing a fresh towel. She said I should wash. I took the towel
from her and put it beside me. Mona came in unwillingly. She
sat down and tried to endure me so near. She spread her napkin
and my mother brought in a bowl of soup. But the smell was
too much for Mona. The sight of the soup revolted her. She
grabbed the pit of her stomach, threw down her napkin and left
the table.

"I can't *do* it. I just can't!"

"Haw! Weaklings. Females. Bring on the food!"

Then my mother left. I ate alone. When I was through
I lit a cigarette and sat back to give the women some thought.
My thought was to find the best possible way to destroy them.

There was no doubt of it: they had to be finished. I could burn them, or cut them to pieces, or drown them. At last I decided that drowning would be the best. I could do it in comfort while I took my bath. Then I would toss the remains down the sewer. They would flow down to the sea, where the dead crabs lay. The souls of the dead women would talk to the souls of the dead crabs, and they would talk only of me. My fame would increase. Crabs and women would arrive at one inevitable conclusion: that I was a terror, the Black Killer of the Pacific Coast, yet a terror respected by all, crabs and women alike: a cruel hero, but a hero nevertheless.

TWELVE

After supper I turned on the water for my bath. I was contented from food and in a fine mood for the execution. The warm water would make it even more interesting. While the tub was filling I entered my study, locking the door behind me. Lighting the candle, I lifted the box which concealed my women. There they lay huddled together, all my women, my favorites, thirty women chosen from the pages of art magazines, women not real, but good enough nevertheless, the women who belonged to me more than any real women could ever belong to me. I rolled them up and stuck them under my shirt. I had to do this. Mona and my mother were in the living room and I had to pass them to get into the bathroom.

So this was the end! Destiny had brought this! The very thought of it! I looked around the closet and tried to feel sentimental. But it wasn't very sad: I was too eager to go ahead with the execution to be sad. But just for the sake of formality I stood still and bowed my head as a token of farewell. Then I blew out the candle and stepped into the living room. I left the door open behind me. It was the first time I ever left the door open. In the living room sat Mona, sewing. I crossed the rug, a slight bulge under my waist. Mona looked up and saw the open door. She was greatly surprised.

"You forgot to lock your study,' " she sneered.

"I know what I'm about, if you please. And I'll lock that door whenever I damn well feel like it."

"But what about Nietzsche, or whatever you call him?"

"Never mind Nietzsche, you Comstock trull."

The tub was ready. I undressed and sat in it. The pictures lay face down on the bath mat, within range of my hand.

I reached down and picked off the top picture.

For some reason I knew it was going to be Helen. A faint instinct told me so. And Helen it was. Helen, dear Helen! Helen with her light brown hair! I had not seen her for a long time, almost three weeks. A strange thing about Helen, that strangest of women: the only reason I cared for her was because of her long fingernails. They were so pink, such breath-taking fingernails, so sharp and exquisitely alive. But for the rest of her I cared nothing, beautiful though she was throughout. She sat naked in the picture, holding a soft veil about her shoulders, every bit a marvelous sight, yet not interesting to me, except for those beautiful fingernails.

"Goodbye, Helen," I said. "Goodbye, dear heart. I shall never forget you. Until the day I die I shall always remember the many times we went to the deep corn-fields of Anderson's book and I went to sleep with your fingers in my mouth. How delicious they were! How sweetly I slept! But now we part, dear Helen, sweet Helen. Goodbye, goodbye."

I tore the picture to pieces and floated them on the water.

Then I reached down again. It was Hazel. I had named her so because of her eyes in a picture of natural colors. Yet I didn't care for Hazel either. It was her hips I cared about — they were so pillowy and so white. What times we had had, Hazel and I! How beautiful she really was! Before I destroyed her I lay back in the water and thought of the many times we had met in a mysterious room pierced with dazzling sunlight, a very white room, with only a green carpet on the floor, a room that existed only because of her. In the corner, leaning against the wall, and for no good reason, but always there, a long slender cane with a silver tip, flashing diamonds in the sunlight. And from behind a curtain that I never quite saw because of the mistiness, and yet could never quite deny, Hazel would walk in such a melancholy way to the middle of the room, and I would be there admiring the globed beauty of her hips, on my knees before her, my fingers melting for the touch of her, and yet I never spoke to darling Hazel but to her hips, addressing them as though they were living souls, telling them how wonderful they were, how useless life was without them, the while taking them in my hands and drawing them near me. And I tore that picture to pieces too, and watched the pieces absorb the water. Dear Hazel. . . .

Then there was Tanya. I used to meet Tanya at night in a cave we kids built one summer a long time ago along the Palos Verdes Cliffs near San Pedro. It was near the sea, and you could smell the ecstasy of lime trees growing there. The cave was always strewn with old magazines and newspapers. In one corner lay a frying pan I had stolen from my mother's kitchen, and in another corner a candle burned and made hissing noises. It was really a filthy little cave after you had been there a little while, and very cold, for water dripped from the sides. And there I met Tanya. But it was not Tanya I loved. It was the way she wore a black shawl in the picture. And it wasn't the shawl either. One was incomplete without the other, and only Tanya could wear it that way. Always when I met her I found myself crawling through the opening of the cave to the center of the cave and pulling the shawl away as Tanya's long hair fell loosely about her, and then I would hold the shawl to my face and bury my lips in it, admiring its black brilliance, and thanking Tanya over and over for having worn it again for me. And Tanya would always answer,

"But it's nothing, you silly. I do it gladly. You're so silly." And I would say, "I love you, Tanya."

There was Marie. Oh Marie! Oh you Marie! You with your exquisite laughter and deep perfume! I loved her teeth and mouth and the scent of her flesh. We used to meet in a dark room whose walls were covered by cobwebbed books. There was a leather chair near the fireplace, and it must have been a very great house, a castle or a mansion in France, because across the room, big and solid, stood the desk of Emile Zola as I had seen it in a book. I would be sitting there reading the last pages of *Nana*, that passage about the death of Nana, and Marie would rise like a mist from those pages and stand before me naked, laughing and laughing with a beautiful mouth and an intoxicating scent until I had to put the book down, and she walked before me and laid her hands on the book too, and shook her head with a deep smile, so that I could feel her warmth coursing like electricity through my fingers.

"Who are you?"

"I am Nana."

"Really Nana?"

"Really."

"The girl who died here?"

"I am not dead. I belong to you."

And I would take her in my arms.

There was Ruby. She was an erratic woman, so unlike the others, and so much older too. I always came upon her as she ran across a dry hot plain beyond the Funeral Range in Death Valley, California. That was because I had been there once in the spring, and I never forgot the beauty of that vast plain, and there it was I met the erratic Ruby so often afterward, a woman of thirty-five, running naked across the sand, and I chasing after her and finally catching her beside a pool of blue water which always gave off a red vapor the moment I dragged her into the sand and sank my mouth against her throat, which was so warm

and not so lovely, because Ruby was growing old and cords protruded slightly, but I was mad about her throat, and I loved the
touch of her cords rising and falling as she panted where I had
caught her and brought her to the earth.

And Jean! How I loved Jean's hair! It was as golden as
straw, and always I saw her drying the long strands under a
banana tree that grew on a knoll among the Palos Verdes Hills.
I would be watching her as she combed out the deep strands.
Asleep at her feet coiled a snake like the snake under the feet
of the Virgin Mary. I always approached Jean on tiptoe, so as
not to disturb the snake, who sighed gratefully when my feet sank
into him, giving me such an exquisite pleasure everywhere,
lighting up the surprised eyes of Jean, and then my hands slipped
gently and cautiously into the eerie warmth of the golden hair,
and Jean would laugh and tell me she knew it was going to happen
this way, and like a falling veil she would droop into my arms.

But what of Nina? Why did I love that girl? And why was
she crippled? And what was it within my heart that made me
love her so madly simply because she was so hopelessly maimed?
Yet it was all so, and my poor Nina was crippled. Not in the
picture, oh she wasn't crippled there, only when I met her, one
foot smaller than the other, one foot like that of a doll, the other
a proper shape. We met in the Catholic church of my boyhood,
St. Thomas's in Wilmington, where I, dressed in the robes of a
priest, stood with a scepter at the high altar. All around me on
their knees were the sinners, weeping after I had castigated them
for their sins, and not one of them had the courage to look upon
me because my eyes shone with such mad holiness, such a detesta-
tion of sin. Then from the back of the church came this girl, this
cripple, smiling, knowing she was going to break me from my
holy throne and force me to sin with her before the others, so
that they could mock me and laugh at me, the holy one, the
hypocrite before all the world. Limping she came, disrobing at
every painful step, her wet lips a smile of approaching triumph,

and I with the voice of a falling king, shouting to her to go away, that she was a devil who bewitched me and made me helpless. But she came forward irresistibly, the crowd horror-stricken, and she put her arms around my knees and hugged me to her, hiding that crippled little foot, until I could endure it no longer, and with a shout I fell upon her and joyfully admitted my weakness while around me rose the rumble of a mob which gradually faded into a bleak oblivion.

And so it was. So it was that one by one I picked them up, remembered them, kissed them good-bye, and tore them to pieces. Some were reluctant to be destroyed, calling in pitiful voices from the misty depths of those vast places where we loved in weird half-dreams, the echoes of their pleas lost in the shadowed darkness of that which was Arturo Bandini as he sat comfortably in a cool bathtub and enjoyed the departure of things which once were, yet never were, really.

But there was one in particular which I was loath to destroy. She alone caused me to hesitate. She it was whom I had named the Little Girl. She it seemed was always that woman of a certain murder case in San Diego; she had killed her husband with a knife and laughingly admitted the crime to the police. I used to meet her in the rough squalor of early Los Angeles before the days of the Gold Rush. She was very cynical for a little girl, and very cruel. The picture I had cut from the detective magazine left nothing to imagine. Yet she wasn't a little girl at all. I merely called her that. She was a woman who hated the sight of me, the touch of me, yet found me irresistible, cursing me, yet loving me fabulously. And I would see her in a dark mud-thatched hut with the windows darkened, the heat of the town driving all the natives to sleep so that not a soul stirred in the streets of that early day of Los Angeles, and lying on a cot she would be, panting and cursing me as my feet sounded upon the deserted street and finally at her door. The knife in her hand would amuse me and make me smile, and so would her hideous screams. I was such a devil. Then my smile would leave her helpless, the hand that held the knife finally growing limp, the knife falling to the floor, and she cringing in horror and hate, yet wild with love. So she was the Little Girl, and of them all she was easily my favorite. I regretted destroying her. For a long time I deliberated, because I knew she would find relief and surcease from me once I destroyed her, because then I could no longer harass her like a devil, and possess her with contemptible laughter. But the Little Girl's destiny was sealed. I could play no favorites. I tore the Little Girl to pieces like the others.

When the last had been destroyed the pieces blanketed the surface of the water, and the water was invisible beneath. Sadly I stirred it up. The water was a blackish color of fading ink. It was finished. The show was over. I was glad I had made this bold step and put them away all at once. I congratulated myself for having such strength of purpose, such ability to see a job through to the end. In the face of sentimentality I had gone ruthlessly forward. I was a hero, and my deed was not to be sneered at. I stood up and looked at them before I pulled the plug. Little pieces of departed love. Down the sewer with the romances of Arturo Bandini! Go down to the sea! Be off on your dark journey down the drain to the land of dead crabs. Bandini had spoken. Pull the chain!

And it was done. I stood with water dripping from me and saluted.

"Goodbye," I said. "Farewell, ye women. They laughed at me down at the cannery today, and it was the fault of ye, for ye hath poisoned my mind and made me helpless against the onslaught of life. Now ye are dead. Goodbye and goodbye forever. He who maketh a sap of Arturo Bandini, be he man or woman, cometh to an untimely end. I have spoken. Amen."

THIRTEEN

Asleep or awake, it did not matter, I hated the cannery, and I always smelled like a basket of mackerel. It never left me, that stench of a dead horse at the edge of the road. It followed me in the streets. It went with me into buildings. When I crawled into bed at night, there it was, like a blanket, all over me. And in my dreams there were fish fish fish, mackerel slithering about in a black pool, with me tied to a limb and being lowered into the pool. It was in my food and clothes, and I even tasted it on my toothbrush. The same thing happened to Mona and my mother. At last it got so bad that when Friday came we had meat for dinner. My mother couldn't bear the idea of fish, even though it was a sin to be without fish.

From boyhood I loathed soap too. I didn't believe I would ever get used to that slimy greasy stuff with its slithering, effeminate smell. But now I used it against the stench of fish. I took more baths than ever before. There was one Saturday when I took two baths — one after work, and another before I went to bed. Every night I stayed in the tub and read books until the water grew cold and looked like old dish water. I rubbed soap into my skin until it shone like an apple. But there was no sense in it all, because it was a waste of time. The only way to get rid of the smell was to quit the cannery. I always left the tub smelling of two mingling stenches — soap and dead mackerel.

Everybody knew who I was and what I did when they smelled me coming. Being a writer was no satisfaction. On the bus I was recognized instantly, and in the theatre too. He's one of those cannery kids. Good Lord, can't you smell him? I had that well-known smell.

One night I went to the theatre to see a picture show. I sat by myself, all alone in the corner, my smell and I. But distance was a ridiculous obstacle to that thing. It left me and went out and around and returned like something dead fastened to a rubber band. In a while heads began to turn. A cannery worker was somewhere in the vicinity, obviously. There were frowns and sniffs. Then mumbling, and the scraping of feet. People all around me got up and moved away. Keep away from him, he's a cannery worker. And so I went to no more picture shows. But I didn't mind. They were for the rabble anyhow.

At night I stayed home and read books.

I didn't dare go to the library.

I said to Mona, "Bring me books by Nietzsche. Bring me the mighty Spengler. Bring me Auguste Comte and Immanuel Kant. Bring me books the rabble can't read."

Mona brought them home. I read them all, most of them very hard to understand, some of them so dull I had to pretend they were fascinating, and others so awful I had to read them aloud like an actor to get through them. But usually I was too tired for reading. A little while in the bathtub was enough. The print floated near my eyes like thread in the wind. I fell asleep. Next morning I found myself undressed and in bed, the alarm ringing, wondering how my mother had not waked me up. And as I dressed I thought over the books I had read the night before. I could remember only a sentence here and there, and the fact that I had forgotten everything.

I even read a book of poetry. It made me sick, that book, and I said I would never read another again. I hated that poet. I wished she would spend a few weeks in a cannery. Then her tune would change.

Most of all, I thought about money. I never did have much money. The most I ever had at one time was fifty dollars. I used to roll paper in my hands and pretend it was a wad of thousand dollar bills. I stood in front of a mirror and peeled it off to clothiers, automobile salesmen, and whores. I gave one whore a thousand dollar tip. She offered to spend the next six months with me for nothing. I was so touched I peeled off another thousand and gave it to her for sentiment's sake. At this she promised to give up her bad life. I said tut tut, my dear, and gave her the rest of the roll: seventy thousand dollars.

A block from our apartment was the California Bank. I used to stand at our window at night and see it bulging out so insolently on the corner. I finally thought of a way to rob it without being caught. Next door to the bank was a dry-cleaner establishment. The idea was to dig a tunnel from the dry cleaner's to the bank safe. A getaway car could be waiting in back. It was only a hundred miles to Mexico.

If I didn't dream of fish I dreamed of money. I used to wake up with my fist clenched, thinking there was money in it, a gold piece, and hating to open my hand because I knew my mind was playing a trick, and there was really no money at all in my hand. I made a vow that if I ever got enough money I would buy the Soyo Fish Company, have an all night celebration like the Fourth of July, and burn it to the ground in the morning.

The work was hard. In the afternoons the fog lifted and the sun beat down. The rays lifted themselves from the blue bay inside the saucer formed by the Palos Verdes hills and it was like a furnace. In the cannery it was worse. There was no fresh air, not even enough to fill one nostril. All the windows were nailed down by rusted nails, and the glass was cobwebbed and greasy with age. The sun heated the corrugated iron roof like a torch, forcing the heat downward. Hot steam drifted from the retorts and ovens. More steam came from the big fertilizer vats. These two steams met head on, you could see them meeting, and we were right in the middle of it, sweating in the clamor of the can dump.

My uncle was right about the work, all right. It was work done without thinking. You might just as well have left your brains at home on that job. All we did through the whole day was stand there and move our arms and legs. Once in a while we shifted weight, one foot to the other. If you really wanted to move, you had to leave the platform to go to the water fountain or the lavatory. We had a plan: we took turns: each of us took ten minutes in the lavatory by turn. No boss was necessary with those machines working. When the labeling began in the morning Shorty Naylor threw the switch and left the room. He knew about those machines. We didn't like to see them get ahead of us. When they did it hurt us vaguely. It was not a pain like someone jabbing you in the seat with a pin, but it was a sadness which in the long run was worse. If we escaped there was always someone down the line who didn't. He yelled. Up in front we had to work harder to fill up the space in the conveyor belt so he would feel better. Nobody liked that machine. It didn't matter if you were a Filipino or an Italian or a Mexican. It bothered us all. It needed such care too. It was like a child. Whenever it broke down panic would go through the whole cannery. Everything was done to the minute. When the machines were silenced it was like another place. It was no longer a cannery but a hospital. We waited around, talking in whispers until the mechanics fixed it.

I worked hard because I had to work hard, and I didn't complain much because there wasn't any time to complain. Most of the time I stood feeding the machine and thinking of money and women. Time passed easier with such thoughts. It was the first job I ever had where, the less you thought about your work, the easier it was. I used to get very passionate with my thoughts of women. That was because the platform was in a state of perpetual jerking. One dream of them slipped into another, and the hours passed away as I stood close to the machine and tried to concentrate on my work so the other boys wouldn't know what I was thinking about.

Through the haze of steam I could see across the room to the open door. There lay the blue bay swept by hundreds of dirty lazy gulls. On the other side of the bay was the Catalina Dock. Every few minutes in the morning steamers and airplanes left the dock for Catalina Island, eighteen miles away. Through the hazy door I could see the red pontoons of the planes as they lifted from the water. The steamers left only in the mornings, but all day long the planes soared away to the little island eighteen miles away. The dripping red pontoons flashed in the sunlight, frightening the gulls. But from where I stood I could only see the pontoons. Only the pontoons. Never the wings and fuselage.

This upset me from the first day. I wanted to see the whole plane. Many times I had seen the planes on my way to work. I used to stand on the bridge and watch the pilots tinker with them, and I knew every plane in the fleet. But seeing only the pontoons through the door, it worked on my mind like a bug. I used to think the craziest things. I used to imagine things were happening to the invisible parts of the plane — that stowaways were riding the wings. I wanted to rush to the door to make sure. I was always having hunches. I used to wish for tragedies. I wanted to see the planes blow up and the passengers drown in the bay. Some mornings I would come to work with only one hope in mind — that somebody would be killed in the bay. I used to be convinced of it. The next plane, I would say, the next one will never get to Catalina: it will crash in the take-off; people will scream, women and children will drown in the bay; Shorty Naylor will throw the switch and we will all get to see the rescuers pull the bodies out of the water. It is bound to happen. It is inevitable. And I used to think I was psychic. And so, all day long the planes pulled away. But standing where I was, all I saw was the pontoons. My bones ached to break away. The *next* one would surely crash. I made noises in my throat, biting my lips and waiting feverishly for that next plane. Presently I heard the roar of the motors, faint above the cannery din, and I timed it. Death at last! Now they will die! When the time arrived, I stopped work and stared, hungry for the sight. The planes never varied an inch in the take-off. The perspective through the door never changed. This time, as always, all I saw were the pontoons. I sighed. Ah well, who knows? Maybe it will crash beyond the lighthouse at the end of the breakwater. I will know in a minute. The coast guard sirens will sound. But the sirens didn't sound. Another plane had got through.

Fifteen minutes later I heard the roar of another plane. We were supposed to stay there. But the devil with orders. I jumped from the can dump and ran to the door. The big red plane took off. I saw all of it, every inch of it, and my eyes made a little feast before the tragedy. Out there, anywhere, lurked death. At any moment he would strike. The plane moved across the bay, shot into the air, and moved toward the San Pedro lighthouse. Smaller and smaller. It had escaped too. I shook my fist at it.

"You'll get it yet!" I screamed.

The boys at the can dump watched me in amazement. I felt like a fool. I turned around and returned. Their eyes accused me, as if I had run to the door and tried to kill a beautiful bird.

All at once I had a different view of them. They looked so stupid. They worked so hard. With wives to feed, and a swarm of dirty-faced kids, and worries about the light bill and the grocery bill, they stood so far away, so detached, naked in dirty overalls, with stupid, pock-marked Mexican faces, glutted with stupidity, watching me return, thinking me crazy, making me shiver. They were gobs of something sticky and slow, gobby and glutted and in the way like glue, gluey and stuck and helpless and hopeless, with the whipped sad eyes of old animals from a field. They thought me crazy because I didn't look like an old whipped animal from a field. Let them think me crazy! Of course I'm crazy! You clod-hoppers, you dolts, you fools! I don't care about your thoughts. I was disgusted that I had to be so near them. I wanted to beat them up, one at a time, beat them until they were a mass of wounds and blood. I wanted to yell at them to keep their god-damn mopey melancholy whipped eyes away from me, because they turned a black slab in my heart, an open place, a grave, a hole, a sore, out of which marched in a torturing procession their dead leading other dead after them, parading the bitter suffering of their lives through my heart.

The machine clanged and banged. I took my place beside Eusibio and worked, the same routine, feeding the cans to the machine, resigned to the fact that I was not psychic, that tragedy only struck like a coward in the night. The boys watched me begin again, then they began too, giving me up for a maniac. Nothing was said. The minutes passed. It was an hour later.

Eusibio nudged me.

"For why you run like that?"

"The pilot. An old friend of mine. Colonel Buckingham. I was waving to him."

Eusibio shook his head.

"Bull, Arturo. You full of bull."

FOURTEEN

From my place on the conveyor I could also see the California Yacht Club. In the background were the first green ripples of the Palos Verdes Hills. It was a scene out of the Italy I knew in books. Bright pennants flapped from the masts of yachts. Farther out were the whitecaps of the big waves that smashed against the jagged breakwater. On the decks of the yachts, lay men and women in careless white suits. These were fabulous people. They were from the movie colony and Los Angeles financial circles. They had great wealth, these boats were their toys. If they felt like it they left their work in the city and came down to the harbor to play with them, and brought along their women.

And such women! It took my breath away to even see them rolling by in big cars, so poised, so beautiful, so easily at home in all that wealth, their cigarettes tipped so elegantly, their teeth so polished and flashing, the clothes they wore so irresistible, covering them with such perfection, concealing every body flaw, and making them so perfect in loveliness. At noon when the big cars roared down the road past the cannery and we were outside for the lunch hour I used to look at them like a thief peeking at jewels. Yet they seemed so far away that I hated them, and hating them made them nearer. Some day they would be mine. I would own them and the cars that carried them. When the revolution came they would be mine, the subjects of Commissar Bandini, right there in the Soviet district of San Pedro.

But I remember a woman on a yacht. She was two hundred yards away. At that distance I could not see her face. Only her movements were plain as she walked the deck like a pirate queen in a brilliant white bathing suit. She walked up and down the deck of a yacht that stretched like a lazy cat in the blue water. It was only a memory, an impression to be got from standing at the can dump and looking out the door. Only a memory, but I fell in love with her, the first real woman I ever loved. Occasionally she paused at the rail to look down into the water. Then she walked again, her luxurious thighs moving up and down. Once she turned and stared at the sprawling cannery. For some minutes she stared. She could not see me, but she looked directly at me. In that instant I fell in love with her. It must have been love, and yet it might have been her white bathing suit. From all angles I considered it, finally admitting that it was love. After looking at me, she turned and paced again. I am in love, I said. So this is love! All day I thought about her. The next day the yacht was gone. I used to wonder about her, and though it never seemed important, I was sure I was in love with her. After a while I ceased to think of her, she became a memory, a mere thought to while away the hours at the can dump. I loved her though; she never saw me, and I never saw her face, but it was love for all that. I couldn't make myself believe I had loved her either, but I decided that for once I was wrong, and that I did love her.

Once a beautiful blonde girl entered the labeling room.

She came with a man who had an elegant mustache and wore spats. Later I found out his name was Hugo. He owned the cannery, as well as one on Terminal Island and another in Monterey. Nobody knew who the girl was. She clung to his arm, sickened by the odor. I knew she didn't like the place. She was a girl of not more than twenty. She wore a green coat. Her back was perfectly arched, like a barrel stave, and she wore high white shoes. Hugo was examining the place coldly, appraising it. She whispered to him. He smiled and patted her arm. Together they walked away. At the door the girl turned to look at us. I put my head down, not wanting to be seen by one so lovely among those Mexicans and Filipinos.

Eusibio was next to me on the can dump.

He nudged me and said, "You like, Arturo?"

"Don't be a fool," I said. "She's a slut, pure and simple, a capitalistic slut. Her day is finished when the revolution comes."

But I never forgot that little girl with her green coat and high white shoes. I was sure I would meet her again some day. Perhaps after I became rich and famous. Even then I wouldn't know her name, but I would hire detectives to shadow Hugo until they came to the apartment where he kept her, a virtual prisoner in his stupid wealth. The detectives would come to me with the address of the place. I would go there and present my card.

"You don't remember me," I would smile.

"Why no. I'm afraid not."

Ah. Then I would tell her of that visit she made to the Soyo Fish Company in the years gone by. How I, a poor white lad among that pack of ignorant Mexicans and Filipinos, was so overcome by her beauty that I dared not show my face. Then I would laugh.

"But of course you know who I am now."

I would lead her to her book shelf, where my own books were to be seen among a few indispensable others, such as the bible and the dictionary, and I would draw out my book

Colossus of Destiny, the book for which I had been given the Nobel Award.

"Would you like me to autograph it?"

Then, with a gasp, she would know.

"Why, you're Bandini, the famous Arturo Bandini!"

Haw. And I would laugh again.

"In the flesh!"

What a day! What a triumph!

FIFTEEN

A month passed, with four pay checks. Fifteen dollars a week.

I never got used to Shorty Naylor. For that matter, Shorty Naylor never got used to me. I couldn't talk to him, but he couldn't talk to me either. He was not a man to say, Hello, how are you? He merely nodded. And he wasn't a man to discuss the canning situation or world politics. He was too cold. He kept me at a distance. He made me feel as if I were an employee. I already knew I was an employee. I didn't see any need to rub it in.

The end of the mackerel season was in sight. An afternoon came when we finished labeling a two hundred ton batch. Shorty Naylor appeared with a pencil and a checking board. The mackerel were boxed, stenciled, and ready to go. A freighter was moored at the docks, waiting to carry them off to Germany – a wholesale house in Berlin.

Shorty gave the word for us to move the shipment out on the docks. I wiped the sweat from my face as the machine came to a stop, and with easy good-nature and tolerance I walked over to Shorty and slapped him on the back.

"How's the canning situation, Naylor?" I said. "What sort of competition do we get from those Norwegians?"

He shook the hand from his shoulder.

"Get yourself a hand truck and go to work."

"A harsh master," I said. "You're a harsh master, Naylor."

I took a dozen steps and he called my name. I returned.

"Do you know how to work a hand truck?"

I had no thought of it. I didn't even know hand trucks went by such a name. Of course I didn't know how to work a hand truck. I was a writer. Of course I didn't know. I laughed and pulled up my dungarees.

"Very funny! Do *I* know how to work a hand truck! And you ask me that! Haw. Do I know how to work a hand truck!"

"If you don't—say so. You don't have to kid me."

I shook my head and looked at the floor.

"Do *I* know how to work a hand truck! And you ask me that!"

"Well, *do* you?"

"Your question is patently absurd on the face of it. Do I know how to work a hand truck! Of course I know how to work a hand truck. Naturally!"

His lip curled like a rat's tail.

"Where did *you* ever learn to work a hand truck?"

I spoke to the room at large. "Now he wants to know where I worked a hand truck! Imagine that! He wants to know where I learned to work a hand truck."

"All right, we're wasting time. Where? I'm asking you where?"

Like a rifle report I responded.

"The docks. The gasoline docks. Stevedoring."

His eyes crawled over me from head to foot, and his lip took several weary curls, a man utterly nauseated with contempt.

"*You* a stevedore!"

He laughed.

I hated him. The imbecile. The fool, the dog, the rat, the skunk. The skunk-faced rat. What did he know about it. A lie, yes. But what did he know about it? Him—this rat—with not one ounce of culture, who had probably never read a book in his life. My God! What could he ever know about anything? And another thing. He wasn't so big either, with his missing teeth and tobacco-juice mouth and eyes of a boiled rat.

"Well," I said. "I've been looking you over, Saylor or Taylor, or Naylor, or whatever the hell they call you down here in this stink-hole, I don't give a damn myself; and unless my perspective is completely awry, you're not so goddamn big yourself, Saylor, or Baylor, or Taylor, or Naylor, or whatever the hell your name is."

A foul word, too foul to repeat, oozed out of the side of his face. He scratched his checking board, making some sort of pretense not clear to me, but plainly a form of hypocrisy, a ruse from the depths of his brummagem soul, scratching away like a rat, an uncultured rat, and I hated him so much I could have bitten off his finger and spat it in his face. Look at him! That rat, making ratty little scratches on a piece of paper like a piece of cheese with his ratty little paws, the rodent, the pig, the alley rat, the dock rat. But why didn't he say something? Ha. Because at last he had found his match in me, because he was helpless before his betters.

I nodded at the stack of cartoned mackerel.

"I see this stuff is bound for Germany."

"No fooling?" he said, scratching away.

But I didn't flinch under this plodding effort to be sarcastic. The witticism found no target upon me. Instead, I lapsed into a serious silence.

"Say Naylor, or Baylor, or whatever it is — what do you think of modern Germany? Do you agree with Hitler's Weltanschauung?"

No response. Not a word, merely a scratching. And why not? Because Weltanschauung was too much for him! Too much for any rat. It baffled, stupefied him. It was the first time and the last he would ever hear the word uttered in his life. He put the pencil in pocket and peered over my shoulder. He had to get up on his tiptoes to do it, he was such a preposterously dwarfed little runt.

"Manuel!" he called. "Oh Manuel! Come here a minute."

Manuel came forward, scared, halting, because it was unusual for Shorty to address anybody by name, unless he was going to sack him. Manuel was thirty, with a hungry face and cheek bones protruding like eggs. He worked across from me on the can dump. I used to look at him a lot because of his huge teeth. They were as white as milk, but too big for his face, his upper lip not long enough to cover them. He made me think of teeth, and nothing else.

"Manuel, show this fellow how to work a hand truck."

I interrupted. "It's scarcely necessary, Manuel. But under the circumstances, he gives the orders around here and, as they say, an order is an order."

But Manuel was on Shorty's side.

"Come on," he said. "I show you."

He led me away, the foul words oozing from Shorty's mouth again, easy to hear.

"This amuses me," I said. "It's funny, you know. I feel like laughing. That poltroon."

"I show you. Come on. Boss's orders."

"The boss is a moron. He's dementia praecox."

"No no! Boss's orders. Come on."

"Very amusing in a macabre way—right out of Krafft-Ebing."

"Boss's orders. Can't help."

We went to the room where they were kept, and each of us dragged out a hand truck. Manuel pushed his into the clear. I followed. This was easy enough. So they were called hand trucks. When I was a kid we called them pushcarts. Anybody with two hands could work a hand truck. The back of Manuel's head was like the fur of a black cat shaved by a rusty butcher-knife. The growth was like a cliff: it was a home-made hair cut. The seat of his overalls was patched with a hunk of white canvas. It was badly sewed, as if he had used a hair pin and a length of string. His heels were worn down to the wet floor, the soles re-soled with wet fiber, held together by big nails. He looked so poor it made me mad. I knew a lot of poor people, but Manuel didn't have to be *that* poor.

"Say," I said. "How much do you make, for God's sake?"

The same as I. Twenty-five cents an hour.

He looked straight into my eyes, a tall lean man looking down, ready to fall apart, with deep dark honest eyes, but very suspicious. They had that whipped, melancholy cast of most all peon eyes.

He said, "You like cannery work?"

"It amuses me. It has its moments."

"I like. I like very much."

"Why don't you get some new shoes?"

"No can afford."

"You married?"

He nodded fast and hard, tickled to be married.

"Got any kids?"

And he was tickled about that too. He had three kids, because he raised three twisted fingers and grinned.

"How the hell do you live on two bits an hour?"

He didn't know. Lord, he didn't know, but he got by. He put his hand on his forehead and made a hopeless gesture. They lived, it wasn't much, but one day followed another and they were alive to see it.

"Why don't you ask for more money?"

He shook his head violently.

"Maybe get fired."

"Do you know what you are?" I said.

No. He didn't know.

"You're a fool. A plain, unmitigated, goddamn fool. Look

at yourself! You belong to the slave-dynasty. The heel of the ruling classes in your groin. Why don't you be a man and go on strike?"

"No strike. No no. Get fired."

"You're a fool. A damn fool. Look at yourself! You haven't even got a decent pair of shoes. And look at your overalls! And by God, you even look hungry. Are you hungry?"

He wouldn't talk.

"Answer me, you fool! Are you hungry?"

"No hungry."

"You dirty liar."

His eyes dropped to his feet as he shuffled along. He was studying his shoes. Then he glanced at mine, which were better than his in every way. He seemed to be happy because I had the best shoes. He looked at my face and smiled. It made me furious. What was the sense in being glad about it? I wanted to punch him.

"Pretty good," he said. "How much you pay?"

"Shut your face."

We went along, I following him. All at once I got so mad I couldn't keep my mouth shut. "You fool! You laissez faire fool! Why don't you pull this cannery down and demand your rights? Demand shoes! Demand milk! Look at yourself! Like a boob, a convict! Where's the milk? Why don't you yell for it?"

His arms tensed on the handle-grips. His dark throat cabled with rage. I thought I had gone too far. Maybe there would be a fight. But it wasn't that.

"Keep still!" he hissed. "Maybe we get fired!"

But the place was too noisy, squealing of wheels and thumping of boxes, with Shorty Naylor a hundred feet away at the door busy checking figures and unable to hear us. And when I saw how safe it was, I decided I wasn't through yet.

"What about your wife and kids? Those dear little babes? Demand milk! Think of them dying of hunger while the babes of the rich swim in gallons of milk! Gallons! And why should it be like that? Aren't you a man like other men? Or are you a fool, a nitwit, a monstrous travesty on the dignity that is man's primordial antecedent? Are you listening to me? Or are you turning your ears because the truth stings them and you are too weak and afraid to be other than an ablative absolute, a dynasty of slaves? Dynasty of slaves! Dynasty of slaves! You want to be a dynasty of slaves! You love the categorical imperative! You don't want milk, you want hypochondria! You're a whore, a slut, a pimp, a whore of modern Capitalism! You make me so sick I feel like puking."

"Yeah," he said. "You puke all right. You no writer. You just puke."

"I'm writing all the time. My head swims in a transvaluated phantasmagoria of phrases."

"Bah! You make me puke too."

"Nuts to you! You Brobdingnagian boor!"

He began stacking boxes for his load. With each he grunted, they were so high and hard to reach. He was supposed to be showing me. Hadn't the boss said to watch? Well, I was watching. Wasn't Shorty the boss? Well, I was carrying out orders. His eyes flashed in anger.

"Come on! Work!"

"Don't talk to me, you capitalistic proletarian bourgeois."

The boxes weighed fifty pounds apiece. He stacked them ten high, one above the other. Then he eased the nose of his truck under the stack and pinched the bottom box with clamps at the base of the truck. I had never seen that kind of a truck. I had seen hand trucks, but not hand trucks with clamps.

"Again Progress rears its fair head. The new technic asserts itself even in the humble hand truck."

"Keep still and watch."

With a jerk he lifted the load from the floor and balanced it on the wheels, the handle-bars at shoulder height. It was a trick. I knew I couldn't do it. He wheeled the load away. And yet, if he could do it, he, a Mexican, a man who without doubt had never read a book in his life, who had never even heard of the transvaluation of values, then so could I. He, this mere peon, had trucked ten boxes.

Then what about you, Arturo? Are you going to be outdone by him? No — a thousand times no! Ten boxes. Good. I will truck twelve boxes. Then I got my truck. By that time Manuel was back for another load.

"Too many," he said.

"Shut up."

I pushed my truck toward the stack and opened the clamps. It had to happen. Too hard. I knew it was going to happen. There was no sense in trying to out-do him, I knew it all the time, yet I did it. There was a splintering and a crash. The tier of boxes tumbled like a tower. They went everywhere. The top box was smashed open. Cans leaped from it, their oval shapes running over the floor like frightened puppies.

"Too many!" Manuel shouted. "I tell you. Too damn many!"

I turned around and screamed, "Will you shut your goddamn greaser face, you goddamn Mexican peon of a boot-licking bourgeois proletarian capitalist!"

The fallen stack was in the path of the other truckers. They trucked around it, kicking out of the way the cans that impeded their movement. I knelt down and gathered them up. It was disgusting, with me, a white man, on my knees, picking up cans of fish, while all around me, standing on their feet, were these foreigners.

Soon enough Shorty Naylor saw what happened. He came on the run.

"I thought you knew how to work a hand truck?"

I stood up.

"These aren't hand trucks. These are clamp-trucks."

"Don't argue. Get that mess cleaned up."

"Accidents will happen, Naylor. Rome wasn't built in a day. There's an old proverb from *Thus Spake Zarathustra.* . . ."

He waved his hands.

"For Christ's sake never mind that! Try again. But this time, don't carry so many. Try five boxes at a time until you get the knack of it."

I shrugged. Oh well, what could you do amongst that hot-bed of stupidity? The only thing left was to be brave, to have faith in man's intrinsic decency, and to cling to a belief in the reality of progress.

"You're the boss," I said. "I'm a writer, you know. Without qualification I . . ."

"Never mind that! I know all about that! Everybody knows you're a writer, everybody. But do me a favor, will you?" He was almost pleading. "Try carrying five boxes, will you? Just five. Not six or seven. Just five. Will you do that for me? Take it easy. Don't kill yourself. Just five at a time."

He walked away. The low words rolled under his breath — obscenities meant for me. So that was it! I thumbed my nose at his retreating back. I despised him, a low person, a boob of limited vocabulary, unable to express his own thoughts, however nasty, except through the brummagem medium of foul language. A rat. He was a rat. He was a nasty, evil-tongued rat who knew nothing about Hitler's Weltanschauung.

Pee on him!

I returned to the task of picking up the fallen tins. When they had all been gathered I decided I would get another truck. In the corner I found one unlike the others, a four-wheeler, a sort of wagon with an iron tongue. It was very light with a wide, flat surface. I drew it to where the boys were loading their hand trucks. It created a sensation. They looked at it as though they had never seen it before, exclaiming in Spanish. Manuel scratched his head in disgust.

"What you do now?"

I pulled the truck into place.

"You wouldn't know—you tool of the bourgeoisie."

Then I loaded it. Not with five boxes. Not with ten. And not with twelve. As I continued to stack them up I realized what possibilities lay in this type of truck. When I finally stopped I had thirty-four aboard.

Thirty-four times fifty? How much was that? I took out my notebook and pencil and figured it. Seventeen hundred pounds. And seventeen hundred times ten were seventeen thousand pounds. Seventeen thousand pounds were eight and one half tons. Eight and one half tons an hour were eighty-five tons a day. Eighty-five tons a day were five hundred and ninety-five tons a week. Five hundred and ninety-five tons a week were thirty thousand nine hundred and forty tons a year. At that rate I would carry three hundred and nine thousand four hundred tons a year. Imagine! And the others carried a mere five hundred pounds per load.

"Gangway!"

They stepped aside and I began to pull. The load moved slowly. I tugged backward, facing the load. My progress was slow because my feet slipped on the wet floor. The load was in the midst of things, directly in the path of the other truckers, which caused a little confusion, but not much, both coming and going. Finally the work stopped. All trucks were glutted in the middle of the room, like a downtown traffic jam. Shorty Naylor hurried in. I was tugging hard, grunting and slipping, losing more ground than I was gaining. But it was no fault of mine. It was the fault of the floor, which was too slippery.

"What the hell's going on here?" Shorty yelled.

I relaxed for a moment's rest. He slapped his hand over his forehead and shook his head.

"What're you doing now?"

"Trucking boxes."

"Get it out of the way! Can't you see you're holding up the job?"

"But look at the size of this load! Seventeen hundred pounds!"

"Get it out of the way!"

"This is more than three times as many. . . ."

"I said, get it out of the way!"

The fool. What could I do against such odds?

The rest of the afternoon I trucked five at a time with a two-wheel truck. It was a very unpleasant task. The only white man, the only American, and he trucking but half as much as the foreigners. I had to do something about it. The boys didn't say anything, but every one of them grinned when they passed me with my measly load of five.

At length I found a way out of it. The worker Orquiza pulled a box from the top of the stack, loosening the whole wall of other boxes. With a yell of warning I ran to the wall and pushed it with my shoulder. It wasn't necessary, but I held the wall against my body, my face purpling, as if the wall was about to collapse upon me. The boys quickly broke down the wall. Afterward I held my shoulder and moaned and clinched my teeth. I staggered away, barely able to walk.

"Are you all right?" they asked.

"It's nothing," I smiled. "Don't worry, fellows. I think I dislocated my shoulder, but it's all right. Don't let it worry you at all."

So now, with a dislocated shoulder, there was no reason for them to grin at my load of five.

That night we worked until seven o'clock. The fog held us up. I stayed a few minutes overtime. I was stalling. I wanted to see Shorty Naylor alone. I had a few things I wanted to discuss with him. When the others had gone and the cannery was deserted, a strange, pleasant loneliness fell upon it. I went to Shorty Naylor's office. The door was open. He was washing his hands in that strong soap powder which was half lye. I could smell it. He seemed a part of the strange, vast loneliness of the cannery, he belonged to it, like a girder across the roof. For a moment he seemed sad and soft, a man with many worries, a person like me, like anyone else. At that evening hour, with the building exposing him to vast loneliness, it seemed to me he was a pretty good fellow after all. But I had something on my mind. I knocked on the door. He turned around.

"Hello there. What's your trouble?"

"No trouble at all," I said. "I merely wanted to get your view on a matter."

"Well, shoot the works. What is it?"

"A little matter I tried to discuss with you earlier this afternoon."

He was drying his hands on a black towel.

"I can't remember. What was it about?"

"You were very uncivil about it this afternoon," I said. "Maybe you won't want to discuss it."

"Oh," he smiled. "You know how it is when a man's busy. Sure, I'll discuss it. What's the trouble?"

"Hitler's Weltanschauung. What is your opinion of the Führer's Weltanschauung?"

"What's that?"

"Hitler's Weltanschauung."

"Hitler's what? Weltan — what?"

"Hitler's Weltanschauung?"

"What's that? What's Weltanschauung? You got me there, boy. I don't even know what it means."

I whistled and backed away.

"My God!" I said. "Don't tell me you don't even know what it means!"

He shook his head and smiled. It was not very important

to him; not as important as drying his hands, for instance. He was not at all ashamed of his ignorance — not in the least shocked. In fact, he seemed rather pleased. I tsk-tsk-tsked with my tongue and backed out of the door, smiling hopelessly. This was almost too much for me. What could I do against an ignoramus like that?

"Well, if you don't know, well, I guess you don't know, and I guess there's no sense in trying to discuss it, if you don't know, and, well, it looks as if you don't know, so, well, goodnight, if you don't know. Goodnight. See you in the morning."

He stood so surprised he forgot to keep drying his hands. Then he called suddenly. "Hey!" he called. "What's this all about?"

But I was gone, hurrying through the darkness of the vast warehouse, only the echo of his voice reaching me. On the way out I passed through the wet clammy room where they dumped mackerel, from the fishing boats. But tonight there were no mackerel, the season had just ended, and instead there were tuna, the first real tuna I ever saw in such numbers, the floor littered with them, thousands of them scattered over a carpet of dirty ice, their white corpse-like bellies blundering through the semi-darkness.

Some of them were still alive. You could hear the sporadic slapping of tails. There in front of me flapped the tail of one who was more alive than dead. I dragged him out of the ice. He was bitter cold and still kicking. I carried him as best I could, dragging him too, until I got him upon the cutting table where the women would dress him tomorrow. He was tremendous, weighing almost a hundred pounds, a monster of a fellow from another world, with great strength still left in his body, and a streak of blood coming from his eye, where he had been hooked. Strong as a man, he hated me and tried to break away from the cutting board. I pulled a gutting knife from the board and held it under his white pulsing gills.

"You monster!" I said. "You black monster! Spell Weltanschauung! Go on — *spell* it!"

But he was a fish from another world; he couldn't spell anything. The best he could do was fight for his life, and he was already too tired for that. But even so, he almost got away. I slugged him with my fist. Then I slid the knife under his gill, amused at his helpless gasping, and cut off his head.

"When I said spell Weltanschauung, I meant it!"

I pushed him back among his comrades upon the ice.

"Disobedience means death."

There was no response save the faint flapping of a tail somewhere in the blackness. I wiped my hands on a gunny sack and walked into the street toward home.

SIXTEEN

The day after I destroyed the women I wished I had not destroyed them. When I was busy and tired I did not think of them, but Sunday was a day of rest, and I would loaf around with nothing to do, and Helen and Marie and Ruby and the Little Girl would whisper to me frantically, asking me why I had been so hasty to destroy them, asking me if I did not now regret it. And I did regret it.

Now I had to be satisfied with their memories. But their memories were not good enough. They escaped me. They were unlike the reality. I could not hold them and look at them as I did the pictures. Now I went around all the time wishing I had not destroyed them, and I called myself a dirty stinking Christian for having done it. I thought about making another collection, but that was not so easy. It had taken a long time to gather those others. I couldn't at will go about finding women to equal the Little Girl, and probably never again would there ever in my life be another woman like Marie. They could never be duplicated. There was another thing that prevented me from making another collection. I was too tired. I used to sit around with a book of Spengler or Schopenhauer and always as I read I kept calling myself a fake and a fool, because what I really wanted were those women who were no more.

Now the closet was different, filled with Mona's dresses and the disgusting odor of fumigation. Some nights I thought I could not bear it. I walked up and down the grey carpet thinking how horrible grey carpets were, and biting my fingernails. I couldn't read anything. I didn't feel like reading a book by a great man, and I used to wonder if they were so great after all. After all, were they as great as Hazel or Marie, or the Little Girl? Could Nietzsche compare with the golden hair of Jean? Some nights I didn't think so at all. Was Spengler as great as Hazel's fingernails? Sometimes yes, sometimes no. There was a time and place for everything, but as far as I was concerned I would rather have the beauty of Hazel's fingernails to ten million volumes by Oswald Spengler.

I wanted the privacy of my study again. I used to look at that closet door and say it was a tombstone through which I could never enter again. Mona's dresses! It sickened me. And yet I could not tell my mother or Mona to please move the dresses elsewhere. I couldn't walk up to my mother and say, "Please move those dresses." The words would not come. I hated it. I thought I was becoming a Babbitt, a moral coward.

One night my mother and Mona were not at home. Just for old time's sake I decided to pay my study a visit. A little sentimental journey into the land of yesterday. I closed the door and stood in the darkness and thought of the many times when this little room was my very own, with no part of my sister disturbing it. But it could never be the same again.

In the darkness I put out my hand and felt her dresses hanging from the clothes-hooks. They were like the shrouds of ghosts, like the robes of millions and millions of dead nuns from the beginning of the world. They seemed to challenge me: they seemed to be there only to harass me and destroy the peaceful fantasy of my women who had never been. A bitterness went through me, and it was painful to even remember the other times. By now I had almost forgotten the features of those others.

I twisted my fist into the folds of a dress to keep from crying out. Now the closet had an unmistakable odor of rosaries and incense, of white lilies at funerals, of carpetry in the churches of my boyhood, of wax and tall, dark windows, of old women in black kneeling at mass.

It was the darkness of the confessional, with a kid of twelve named Arturo Bandini kneeling before a priest and telling him he had done something awful, and the priest telling him nothing was too awful for the confessional, and the kid saying he wasn't sure it was a sin, what he had done, but still he was sure nobody else ever did a thing like that because, father, it's certainly funny, I mean, I don't know how to tell it; and the priest finally wheedling it out of him, that first sin of love, and warning him never to do it again.

I wanted to bump my head against the closet wall and hurt myself so much that I would be senseless. Why didn't I throw those dresses out? Why did they have to remind me of Sister Mary Justin, and Sister Mary Leo, and Sister Mary Corita? I guess I was paying the rent in this apartment; I guess I could throw them out. And I couldn't understand why. Something forbade it.

I felt weaker than ever before, because when I was strong I would not have hesitated a moment; I would have bundled those dresses up and heaved them out the window and spat after them. But the desire was gone. It seemed silly to get angry and start heaving dresses about. It was dead and drifted away.

I stood there, and I found my thumb in my mouth. It seemed amazing that it should be there. Imagine. Me eighteen years old, and still sucking my thumb! Then I said to myself, if you're so brave and fearless, why don't you *bite* your thumb? I dare you to bite it! You're a coward if you don't. And I said, oh! Is that so? Well, I'm not either a coward. And I'll prove it!

I bit my thumb until I tasted blood. I felt my teeth against the pliant skin, refusing to penetrate, and I turned my thumb slowly until the teeth cut through the skin. The pain hesitated, moved to my knuckles, up my arm, then to my shoulder and eyes.

I grabbed the first dress I touched and tore it to pieces. Look how strong you are! Tear it to bits! Rip it until there is nothing left! And I ripped it with my hands and teeth and made grunts like a mad dog, rolling over the floor, pulling the dress across my knees and raging at it, smearing my bloody thumb over it, cursing it and laughing at it as it gave way under my strength and tore apart.

Then I started to cry. The pain in my thumb was nothing. It was a loneliness that really ached. I wanted to pray. I had not said a prayer in two years — not since the day I quit high school and began so much reading. But now I wanted to pray again, I was sure it would help, that it would make me feel better, because when I was a kid prayer used to do that for me.

I got down on my knees, closed my eyes and tried to think of prayer-words. Prayer-words were a different kind of word. I never realized it until that moment. Then I knew the difference.

But there were no words. I had to pray, to say some things; there was a prayer in me like an egg. But there were no words.

Surely not those old prayers!

Not the Lord's Prayer, about Our Father who art in Heaven, hallowed be Thy name, Thy kingdom come. . . . I didn't believe that anymore. There wasn't any such thing as heaven; there might be a hell, it seemed very possible, but there wasn't any such thing as heaven.

Not the Act of Contrition, about O my God, I am heartily sorry for having offended Thee, and I detest all my sins. . . . Because the only thing I was sorry about was the loss of my women, and that was something which God emphatically opposed. Or did He? Surely, He must be against that. If I were God I would certainly be against it. God could hardly be in favor of my women. No. Then He was against them. There was Nietzsche, Friedrich Nietzsche. I tried him. I prayed, "Oh dearly beloved Friedrich!" No good. It sounded like I was a homosexual. I tried again. "Oh dear Mr. Nietzsche." Worse. Because I got to thinking about Nietzsche's pictures in the frontispieces of his books. They made him look like a Forty-niner, with a sloppy mustache, and I detested Forty-niners.

Besides, Nietzsche was dead. He had been dead for years. He was an immortal writer, and his words burned across the pages of his books, and he was a great modern influence, but for all that he was dead and I knew it. Then I tried Spengler. I said, "My dear Spengler." Awful. I said, "Hello there, Spengler." Awful. I said, "Listen, Spengler!" Worse. I said, "Well, Oswald, as I was saying. . . ." Brrr. And still worse.

There were my women. They were dead too; maybe I could find something in them. One at a time I tried them out, but it was unsuccessful because as soon as I thought of them it made me wildly passionate. How could a man be passionate and be in prayer? That was scandalous.

After I had thought of so many people without avail I was weary of the whole idea and about to abandon it, when all of a sudden I had a good idea, and the idea was that I should not pray to God or others, but to myself.

"Arturo, my man. My beloved Arturo. It seems you suffer

so much, and so unjustly. But you are brave, Arturo. You remind me of a mighty warrior, with the scars of a million conquests. What courage is yours! What nobility! What beauty! Ah, Arturo, how beautiful you really are! I love you so, my Arturo, my great and mighty god. So weep now, Arturo. Let your tears run down, for yours is a life of struggle, a bitter battle to the very end, and nobody knows it but you, no one but you, a beautiful warrior who fights alone, unflinching, a great hero the likes of which the world has never known."

I sat back on my heels and cried until my sides ached from it. I opened my mouth and wailed, and it felt ah so good, so sweet to cry, so that soon I was laughing with pleasure, laughing and crying, the tears spilling down my face and washing my hands. I could have gone on for hours.

Footsteps in the living room made me stop. The steps were Mona's. I stood up and wiped my eyes, but I knew they were red. Stuffing the torn skirt under my shirt I walked out of the closet. I coughed a little, clearing my throat, to show I was at ease with everything.

Mona didn't know anyone was in the apartment. The lights were out and everything, and she thought the place was deserted. She looked at me in surprise, as if she had never seen me before. I walked a few feet, this way and that, coughing and humming a tune, but still she watched, saying nothing but keeping her eyes glued to me.

"Well," I said. "You critic of life — say something."

Her eyes were on my hand.

"Your finger. It's all . . ."

"It's my finger," I said. "You God-intoxicated nun."

I locked the bathroom door behind me and threw the tattered dress down the air shaft. Then I bandaged my finger. I stood at the mirror and looked at myself. I loved my own face. I thought I was a very handsome person. I had a good straight nose and a wonderful mouth, with lips redder than a woman's, for all her paint and whatnot. My eyes were big and clear, my jaw protruded slightly, a strong jaw, a jaw denoting character and self-discipline. Yes, it was a fine face. A man of judgment would have found much in it to interest him.

In the medicine cabinet I came upon my mother's wedding ring, where she usually left it after washing her hands. I held the ring in the palm of my hand and looked at it in amazement. To think that this ring, this piece of mere metal, had sealed the connubial bond which was to produce me! That was an incredible thing. Little did my father know, when he bought this ring, that it would symbolize the union of man and woman out of which would arrive one of the world's greatest men. How strange it was to be standing in that bathroom and realizing all these things! Little did this piece of stupid metal know its own significance. And yet someday it would become a collector's item of incalculable value. I could see the museum, with people milling about the Bandini heirlooms, the shouting of the auctioneer, and finally a Morgan or a Rockefeller of tomorrow raising his price to twelve million dollars for that ring, simply because it was worn by the mother of Arturo Bandini, the greatest writer the world had ever known.

SEVENTEEN

A half hour passed. I was reading on the divan. The bandage on my thumb stood out clearly. Mona said no more about it though. She was across the room, reading too, and eating an apple. The front door opened. It was my mother, returning from Uncle Frank's house. The first thing she saw was my bandaged finger.

"My God," she said. "What happened?"

"How much money have you got?" I said.

"But your finger! What happened?"

"How much money have you got?"

Her fingers fluttered through her ragged purse as she kept glancing at the bandaged thumb. She was too excited, too frightened to open the purse. It fell on the floor. She picked it up, her knees crackling, her hands going everywhere, groping after the purse lock. Finally Mona got up and took the purse from her. Completely exhausted, and still worried about my thumb, my mother dropped into a chair. I knew her heart was pounding violently. When she got her breath she again asked about the bandage. But I was reading. I didn't answer.

She asked again.

"I hurt it."

"How?"

"How much money have you got?"

Mona counted it, holding the apple between her teeth.

"Three dollars and a bit of change," she mumbled.

"How much change?" I said. "Be specific please. I like precise answers."

"Arturo!" my mother said. "What happened? How did you hurt it?"

"Fifteen cents," Mona answered.

"Your finger!" my mother said.

"Give me the fifteen cents," I said.

"Come and get it," Mona said.

"But Arturo!" my mother said.

"Give it to me!" I said.

"You're not crippled," Mona said.

"Yes he is too crippled!" my mother said. "Look at his finger!"

"It's *my* finger! And give me that fifteen cents — you!"

"If you want it, come and get it."

My mother jumped from her chair and sat down beside me. She began stroking the hair from my eyes. Her fingers were hot, and she was so powdered with talcum she smelled like a baby, like an aged baby. I got up at once. She stretched her arm out to me.

"Your poor finger! Let me see it."

I walked over to Mona.

"Give me that fifteen cents."

She wouldn't. It lay on the table, but she refused to hand it to me.

"There it is. Pick it up, if you want it."

"I want you to hand it to me."

In disgust she snorted.

"You fool!" she said.

I put the coins in my pocket.

"You'll regret this," I said. "As God is my judge, you'll rue this impudence."

"Good," she said.

"I'm getting tired of being a workhorse for a pair of parasitical females. I tell you I've just about reached the apogee of my fortitude. At any minute now I propose to flee this bondage."

"Poo poo poo," Mona sneered. "Why don't you flee now — tonight? It would make everybody happy."

My mother was completely out of it. Distraught and rocking to and fro she could learn nothing about my finger. All evening I had heard her voice only vaguely.

"Seven weeks at the cannery. I'm fed up with it."

"How did you hurt it?" my mother said. "Maybe it's blood-poisoned."

Maybe it was! For a moment I thought this possible. Working in the unsanitary conditions at the cannery, anything was possible. Then perhaps it *was* blood-poisoned. Me, a poor kid working down in that sweat hole, and this was my reward: blood-poisoning! Me, a poor kid working to support two women because I had to do it. Me, a poor kid, never complaining; and now to die of blood-poisoning from conditions down there where

I earned the bread to feed their mouths. I wanted to burst out crying. I swung around and shouted.

"How did I hurt it? I'll tell you how I hurt it! Now you shall know the truth. Now it can be told. You shall know the demoniacal truth of it. I hurt it in a machine! I hurt it slaving my life away in that carnatic jute-mill! I hurt it because the fungus mouths of two parasitical women depended upon me. I hurt it because of the idiosyncrasies of native intelligence. I hurt it because of incipient martyrdom. I hurt it because my destiny would deny me no dogmatism! I hurt it because the metabolism of my days would deny me no recrudescence! I hurt it because I have a brobdingnagian nobility of purpose!"

My mother sat in shame, understanding nothing I said, but sensing what I was trying to say, her eyes down, her lips pouted, looking innocently into her hands. Mona had gone back to her reading, munching her apple and paying no attention. I turned to her.

"Nobility of purpose!" I screamed. "Nobility of purpose! Do you hear me, you nun! Nobility of purpose! But now I weary of all nobility. I am in revolt. I see a new day for America, for me and my fellow-workers down in that jute-mill. I see a land of milk and honey. I visualize, and I say, Hail the new America! Hail. Hail! Do you hear me, you nun! I say hail! Hail! Hail!"

"Poo poo poo," said Mona.

"Don't sneer — you preposterous monster!"

She made a contemptuous noise in her throat, pulled her book about, and now her back was facing me. Then, for the first time, I noticed the book she was reading. It was a brand new library book, with a bright red jacket.

"What's that you're reading?"

No answer.

"I'm feeding your body. I guess I have the right to know who feeds your brains."

No answer.

"So you won't talk!"

I rushed over and tore the book from her hands. It was a novel by Kathleen Norris. My mouth flew open with a gasp as the whole shocking situation revealed itself. So this was how matters stood in my own home! While I sweated my blood and bone away at the cannery, feeding her body, this, this, was what she fed her brains! Kathleen Norris. This was modern America! No wonder the decline of the west! No wonder the despair of the modern world. So this was it! With me, a poor kid, working my fingers to the bone, trying my best to give them a decent family-life, and this, this, was my reward! I tottered, measured the distance to the wall, staggered toward it, fell over backward toward the wall, and drooped there, gasping for breath.

"My God," I moaned. "My God."

"What's the matter?" my mother said.

"Matter! Matter! I'll tell you what's the matter. Look what she's reading! Oh God almighty! Oh God have mercy on her soul! And to think that I'm slaving my life away, me, a poor kid, ripping the very flesh from my fingers, while she sits around reading this disgusting pig-vomit. Oh God, give me strength! Increase my fortitude! Spare me from throttling her!"

And I tore the book to shreds. The pieces dropped on the carpet. I ground them with my heels. I spat on them, drooled on them, cleared my throat and exploded at them. Then I gathered them up, carried them into the kitchen, and heaved them into the garbage can.

"Now," I said. "Try that again."

"That's a library book," Mona smiled. "You'll have to pay for it."

"I'll rot in jail first."

"Here, here!" my mother said. "What's this all about?"

"Where's that fifteen cents?"

"Let me look at your thumb."

"I said, where's that fifteen cents."

"In your pocket," Mona said. "You fool."
And I walked out.

EIGHTEEN

I crossed the schoolyard toward Jim's Place. In my pocket jingled the fifteen cents. The schoolyard was graveled, and my feet echoed upon it. Here is a good idea, I thought, graveled yards in all prisons, a good idea; something worth remembering; if I were the prisoner of my mother and sister, how futile to escape in this noise; a good idea, something to think about.

Jim was in the back of the store, reading a racing form. He had just put in a new liquor shelf. I stopped in front of it to examine the bottles. Some were very pretty, making their contents appear most palatable.

Jim put down his racing form and walked over. Always impersonal, he waited for the other fellow to speak. He was eating a candy bar. This seemed most unusual. It was the first time I ever saw him with anything in his mouth. I didn't like the looks of him either. I tapped the liquor case.

"I want a bottle of booze."

"Hello!" he said. "And how's the cannery job?"

"It's all right, I guess. But tonight I think I'll get drunk. I don't want to talk about the fish cannery."

I saw a small bottle of whiskey, a five ounce bottle with contents like liquid gold. He wanted ten cents for that bottle. It seemed reasonable enough. I asked him if it was good whiskey. He said it was good whiskey.

"The very best," he said

"Sold. I'll take your word and buy it without further comment."

I handed him the fifteen cents.

"No," he said. "Only a dime."

"Help yourself to the extra nickel. It's a tip, a gesture of personal goodwill and fellowship."

With a smile he would not take it. I still held it out, but he put his palm upward and shook his head. I could not understand why he was always refusing my tips. It wasn't that I only offered them rarely; on the contrary, I tried to tip him every time; in fact, he was the only person I ever tipped.

"Let's not start this all over again," I said. "I tell you I always tip. It's a matter of principle with me. I'm like Hemingway. I always do it second-nature."

With a grunt he took it and jabbed it into his jeans.

"Jim, you're a strange man; a quixotic character shot through with excellent qualities. You surpass the best the mob has to offer. I like you because your mind has scope."

This made him fussy. He would rather talk of other things. He pushed the hair from his forehead and ran his hand over the back of his neck, pulling at it as he tried to think of something to say. I unscrewed the bottle and held it up. "Saluti!" And took a swig. I didn't know why I had bought the liquor. It was the first time in my life I ever put out money for the stuff. I hated the taste of whiskey. It surprised me to find it in my mouth, but there it was indeed, and before I knew it the stuff was working, gritty against my teeth and halfway down my throat, kicking and tearing like a drowning cat. The taste was awful, like burning hair. I could feel it way down, doing strange things inside my stomach. I licked my lips.

"Marvelous! You were right. It's marvelous!"

It was in the pit of my stomach, rolling over and over, trying to find a place to lie, and I rubbed hard so the burning on the outside would equalize the burning within.

"Wonderful! Superb! Extraordinary!"

A woman entered the store. From the corner of my eye I got a flash of her as she stepped to the cigarette counter. Then I turned around and looked at her. She was a woman of thirty, maybe more. Her age didn't matter: she was there — that was the important thing. There was nothing striking about her. She was very plain to see, and yet I could feel that woman. Her presence jumped across the room and tore my breath from my throat. It was like a deluge of electricity. My flesh trembled in excitement. I could feel my own breathlessness and the rush of red blood. She wore an old faded purple coat with a fur neckpiece attached. She was not aware of me. She didn't seem aware of herself. She glanced in my direction and then turned and faced the counter. For a flash I saw her white face. It disappeared behind the fur neckpiece and I never saw it again.

But one glance was enough for me. I would never forget that face. It was a sickly white, like the police photographs of a criminal female. Her eyes were starved and grey and big and hunted. Her hair was any color at all. Brown and black, light yet dark: I didn't remember. She ordered a pack of cigarettes by tapping the counter with a coin. She didn't speak. Jim handed her the pack. He didn't feel the woman at all. She was just another customer to him.

I was still staring. I knew I shouldn't stare that much. I didn't care though. I felt that if she would only see my face she would not object. Her furpiece was an imitation squirrel. The coat was old and threadbare at the hem, which reached to her knees. It fit her closely, lifting her figure toward me. Her hose were gun-metal, with streaks where the weave had got loose and run down. Her shoes were blue, with lop-sided heels and frazzled soles. I smiled and stared at her confidently because I was not afraid of her. A woman like Miss Hopkins upset me and made me feel absurd, but not the picture women, for instance, and not a woman like this woman. It was so easy to smile, it was so insolently easy; it was so much fun to feel so obscene. I wanted to say something dirty, something suggestive, like pheew! I can take whatever you've got to offer, you little bitch. But she did not see me. Without turning she paid for her cigarettes, walked out of the store and down Avalon Boulevard toward the sea.

Jim rang up the sale and returned to where I was standing. He started to say something. Without a word to him I walked out. I just walked right out of there and down the street after that woman. She was more than a dozen steps away, hurrying toward the waterfront. I didn't really know I was following her. When I realized it I stopped dead in my tracks and snapped my fingers. Oh! So now you're a pervert! A sex-pervert! Well well well, Bandini, I didn't think it would come to this; I *am* surprised! I hesitated, tearing big slices out of my thumbnail and spitting them out. But I didn't want to think about it. I would rather think about her.

She was not graceful. Her walk was stubborn, brutish; she walked defiantly, as if to say, I dare you to stop me from walking! She walked with a zig-zag too; moving from one side of the wide sidewalk to the other, sometimes at the curbing and sometimes almost bumping the plate glass windows at her left. But no matter how she walked, the figure under the old purple coat rippled and coiled. Her gait was long and heavy. I kept the original distance she maintained between us.

I felt frenzied; deliriously and impossibly happy. There was that smell of the sea, the clean salted sweetness of the air, the cold cynical indifference of the stars, the sudden laughing intimacy of the streets, the brazen opulence of light in darkness, the glowing languor of slitted crescent moon. I loved it all. I felt like squealing, making queer noises, new noises, in my throat. It was like walking naked through a valley of beautiful girls on all sides.

About half a block down the street I suddenly remembered Jim. I turned to see if he had come to his door to learn why I had hurried away. It was a sickly, guilty feeling. But he was not there. The front of his bright little shop was deserted. The length of Avalon Boulevard showed not a sign of life. I looked up at the stars. They seemed so blue, so cold, so insolent, so far away and utterly contemptuous, so conceited. The bright street lamps made the boulevard as light as early twilight.

I crossed the first corner as she reached the front of the theatre in the next block. She was gathering distance, but I allowed it. You shall not escape me, O beautiful lady, I am at your heels and you have no opportunity to elude me. But where are you going, Arturo? Do you realize that you are following a strange woman? You have never done *this* before. What is your motive? Now I was becoming frightened. I thought about those police cruisers. She drew me on. Ah—that was it—I was her prisoner. I felt guilty, but also I felt I was not doing wrong. After all, I am out for a bit of exercise in the night air; I am taking a walk before retiring, Officer. I live over there, Officer. I have lived there over a year, Officer. My Uncle Frank. Do you know him, Officer? Frank Scarpi? Of course, Officer! Everybody knows my Uncle Frank. A fine man. He'll tell you I'm his nephew. No need to book me, under the circumstances.

As I walked along the bandaged thumb slapped against my thigh. I looked down and there it was, that awful white bandage, slapping away with every step, moving with the motion of my arm, a big white ugly lump, so white and glaring, as if every lamp in the street knew of it and why it was there. I was disgusted with it. To think of it! He bit his own thumb until the blood came! Can you imagine a sane man doing that? I tell you he's insane, sir. He's done some strange things, sir. Did I ever tell you about the time he killed those crabs? I think the guy is crazy, sir. I suggest we book him and have his head examined. Then I tore the bandage off and threw it in the gutter and refused to think about it again.

The woman kept widening the distance between us. Now she was a half block away. I couldn't walk faster. I was going along slowly and I told myself to hurry it a bit, but the idea of the police cruisers began to slow me down. The police in the harbor were from the Los Angeles central station; they were very

121

tough cops on a tough beat and they arrested a man first and then told him why he was arrested, and they always appeared from out of the nowhere, never afoot, but in quiet, fast-moving Buicks.

"Arturo," I said, "you're certainly walking into trouble. You will be arrested for a degenerate!"

Degenerate? What nonsense! Can't I go for a walk if I feel like it? That woman up ahead? I don't know a thing about her. This is a free country, by God. Can I help it if she happens to be moving in the same direction as I? If she doesn't like it, let her walk on another street, Officer. This is my favorite street anyhow, Officer. Frank Scarpi is my uncle, Officer. He will testify that I always go for a walk down this street before retiring. After all, this is a free country, Officer.

At the next corner the woman stopped to strike a match against the wall of the bank. Then she lit a cigarette. The smoke hung in the dead air like distorted blue balloons. I sprang to my toes and hurried. When I got to the motionless clouds I lifted myself on tiptoe and drew them down. The smoke from *her* cigarette! Aha.

I knew where her match had fallen. A few steps more and I picked it up. There it lay, in the palm of my hand. An extra-ordinary match. No perceptible difference from other matches, yet an extraordinary match. It was half burned, a sweet-smelling pine match and very beautiful like a piece of rare gold. I kissed it.

"Match," I said. "I love you. Your name is Henrietta. I love you body and soul."

I put it in my mouth and began to chew it. The carbon tasted of a delicacy, a bitter-sweet pine, brittle and succulent. Delicious, ravishing. The very match she had held in her fingers. Henrietta. The finest match I ever ate, Madam. Let me con-gratulate you.

She was moving faster now, clots of smoke in her wake. I drew big draughts of them down. Aha. That movement in her hips was like a ball of snakes. I felt it in my chest and finger tips.

Now we were advancing toward the cafes and pool-halls along the waterfront. The night air plinked with the voices of men and the distant click of pool balls. In front of the Acme stevedores suddenly appeared, pool cues in their hands. They must have heard the click of the woman's heels on the sidewalk, because they came out so suddenly, and now they were out in front, waiting.

She passed along a lane of silent eyes, and they followed her with a slow pivoting of necks, five men lounging in the doorway. I was fifty feet behind. I detested them. One of them, a monster with a bailing hook stuck in his pocket, took the cigar from his mouth and whistled softly. He smiled to the others, cleared his throat, and spat a silver streak across the sidewalk. I detested that ruffian. Did he know there was a city ordinance forbidding expectorating on a sidewalk? Wasn't he aware of the laws of decent society? Or was he merely an illiterate human monster who had to spit and spit and spit for sheer animalism, a loathsome, vicious urge in his body which forced him to belch out his vile spleen whenever he felt like it? If I only knew his name! I would turn him over to the health department and institute suit against him.

Then I reached the front of the Acme. The men watched me pass too, all of them loafing and seeking something to look at. The woman was now in a section where all the buildings were black and vacant, a great lane of black barren depression windows. For a moment she stopped before one of these windows. Then she went on. Something in the window had caught her eyes and detained her.

When I reached the window I saw what it was. It was the window of the only occupied store in the section. A second-hand store, a pawn shop. Now it was long after office hours and the store was closed, the windows piled high with jewelry, tools, typewriters, suitcases and cameras. A sign in the window read:

123

Highest Prices Paid For Old Gold. Because I knew she had read that sign, I read it over and over again. Highest Prices Paid For Old Gold. Highest Prices Paid For Old Gold. Now both of us had read it, she and I — Arturo Bandini and his woman. Wonderful! And had she not peered carefully into the back of the store? Then so would Bandini, for as did Bandini's woman so did Bandini. A small light burned in the back, over a stumpy little safe. The room bulged with second-hand articles. In one corner stood a wire cage behind which was a desk. The eyes of my woman had seen all of this, and I would not forget.

I turned to follow her again. At the next corner she stepped from the curbing just as the stop light signaled green and GO. I came up fast, eager to cross too, but the light changed to red and STOP. The hell with red lights. Love tolerates no barriers. Bandini must get through. On to victory! And I crossed anyhow. She was only twenty feet before me, the curved mystery of her form flooding me. I would soon be upon her. This had not occurred to me.

Well, Bandini; what will you do now?

Bandini does not falter. Bandini knows what to do, don't you Bandini? Of course I do! I am going to speak sweet words to her. I am going to say hello, my beloved! And a beautiful night it is; and would you object if I walked a bit with you? I know some fine poetry, like the Song of Solomon and that long one from Nietzsche about voluptuousness — which do you prefer? Did you know that I was a writer? Yes indeed! I write for Posterity. Let us walk down to the water's edge while I tell you of my work, of the prose for Posterity.

But when I reached her a strange thing took place.

We were abreast of one another. I coughed and cleared my throat. I was about to say, Hello, my good woman. But something jammed in my throat. I could do nothing else. I couldn't even look at her, because my head refused to turn on my neck. My nerve was gone. I thought I was going to faint. I am collapsing, I said; I am in a state of collapse. And then the

124

strange thing happened: I began to run. I picked up my feet, threw
back my head, and ran like a fool. With elbows chugging and
nostrils meeting the salt air I ran like an Olympic runner, a half-
miler sprinting down the home stretch to victory.

What are you doing now, Bandini? Why are you running?

I feel like running. What of it? I guess I can run if I feel
like it, can't I?

My feet clacked on the deserted street. I was picking up
speed. Doors and windows shot past me in amazing style. I never
realized I had such speed. Passing the Longshoremen's Hall at
a fast clip, I took a wide turn into Front Street. The long
warehouses threw black shadows into the road, and among them
was the swift echo of my feet. I was at the docks now, with the
sea across the street, beyond the warehouses.

I was none other than Arturo Bandini, the greatest half-
miler in the history of the American track and field annals. Gooch,
the mighty Dutch champion, Sylvester Gooch, speed demon from
the land of windmills and wooden shoes, was fifty feet ahead
of me, and the mighty Dutchman was giving me the race of my
career. Would I win? The thousands of men and women in the
stands wondered — especially the women, for I was known jok-
ingly among the sport scribes as a "woman's runner," because I
was so tremendously popular among the feminine fans. Now the
stands were cheering in a frenzy. Women threw out their arms
and begged me to win — for America. Come on, Bandini! Come
on Bandini! Oh you Bandini! How we love you! And the women
were worried. But there was nothing to worry about. The situation was well in hand, and I knew it. Sylvester Gooch was tiring;
he couldn't stand the pace. And I was saving myself for those
last fifty yards. I knew I could defeat him. Fear not, my ladies,
you who love me, fear not! The American honors depend upon
my victory, I know this, and when America needs me you will
find me there, in the midst of the fight, eager to give my blood.
With proud beautiful strides I opened up at the fifty yard mark.
My God, look at that man run! Shrieks of joy from the throats

125

of thousands of women. Ten feet from the tape I lunged forward, snapping it a quarter of a second before the mighty Dutchman. Pandemonium in the stands. Newsreel cameramen gathered around me, begging me for a few words. Please, Bandini, *please!* Leaning against the American-Hawaiian docks I panted for breath and smilingly agreed to give the boys a statement. A nice bunch of fellows.

"I want to say hello to my mother," I panted. "Are you there, Mother? Hello! You see, gentlemen, when I was a boy back in California I had a paper route after school. At that time my mother was in the hospital. Every night she was near death. And that's how I learned to run. With the horrible realization that I might lose my mother before finishing with my Wilmington *Gazettes*, I used to run like a madman, finishing my route and then racing five miles to the hospital. And that was my training ground. I want to thank you all, and once more say hello to my mother back in California. Hello, Mother! How's Billy and Ted? And did the dog get well?"

Laughter. Murmurings about my simple native humility. Congratulations.

But after all, there wasn't much satisfaction in defeating Gooch, great victory though it was. Out of breath I was tired of being an Olympic runner.

It was that woman in the purple coat. Where was she now? I hurried back to Avalon Boulevard. She was not in sight. Except for the stevedores in the next block and the circling of moths around street lamps, the boulevard was deserted.

You fool! You've lost her. She is gone forever.

I began a swing around the block in search for her. In the distance I heard the bark of a police dog. That was Herman. I knew all about Herman. He was the mailman's dog. He was a sincere dog; he not only barked, he also bit. Once he had chased me blocks and tore the socks from my ankles. I decided to give up the search. It was growing late anyhow. Some other night

126

I would seek her. I had to be at work early next morning. And so I started for home, walking up Avalon.

I saw the sign again: Highest Prices Paid For Old Gold. It stirred me because she had read it, the woman in the purple coat. She had seen and felt all of this — the store, the glass, the window, the junk inside. She had walked along this very street. This very sidewalk had felt the enchanted burden of her weight. She had breathed this air and smelled that sea. The smoke from her cigarette had mingled with it. Ah, this is too much, too much!

At the bank I touched the place where she had struck a match. There — on my fingertips. Wonderful. A small black streak. Oh streak, your name is Claudia. Oh Claudia, I love you. I shall kiss you to prove my devotion. I looked about. No one was in sight for two blocks. I reached over and kissed the black streak.

I love you, Claudia. I beg you to marry me. Nothing else in life matters. Even my writings, those volumes for posterity, they mean nothing without you. Marry me or I shall go down to the dock and jump off head first. And I kissed again the black streak.

Then I was horrified to notice that the whole of the bank front was covered with the stripes and streaks of thousands and thousands of matches. I spat in disgust.

Her mark must be a unique mark; something like herself, simple and yet mysterious, a match-streak such as the world had never known before. I shall find it if I have to search forever. Do you hear me? Forever and forever. Until I become an old man I shall stand here, searching and searching for the mysterious mark of my love. Others shall not discourage me. Now I begin: a lifetime or a minute, what does it matter?

After less than two minutes I found it. I was sure of its origin. A small mark so faint that it was almost invisible. Only she could have made it. Wonderful. A tiny little mark with the faintest suggestion of a flair at the tail of it, a bit of artistry to it, a mark like a serpent about to strike.

But someone was coming. I heard footsteps on the sidewalk.

He was a very old man with a white beard. He carried a cane and a book and appeared in deep thought. He limped on his cane. His eyes were very bright and small. I ducked inside the archway until he passed by. Then I emerged and showered savage kisses upon the mark. Again I beseech you to marry me. Greater love than this no man hath. The time and tide wait for no man. A stitch in time saves nine. A rolling stone gathers no moss. Marry me!

Suddenly the night shook with a faint coughing. It was that old man. He had gone down the street about fifty yards and turned around. There he was, leaning on his cane and watching me intently.

Shivering with shame I hurried up the street. At the end of the block I turned around. The old man had now moved back to the wall. He was examining it too. Now he was looking after me. I shuddered at the thought of it. Another block and I turned once more. He was still there, that awful old man. I ran the rest of the way home.

NINETEEN

Mona and my mother were already in bed. My mother snored softly. In the living room the davenport was pulled out, my bed made and the pillow loosened. I undressed and got in. The minutes passed. I couldn't sleep. I tried my back and then my side. Then I tried my stomach. The minutes passed. I could hear them ticking away on the clock in my mother's bedroom. A half hour passed. I was wide awake. I rolled about and felt an ache in my mind. Something was wrong. An hour passed. I began to get angry that I could not sleep, and I started to sweat.

I kicked off the covers and lay there, trying to think of something. I had to get up early. I would be no good at the cannery without a lot of rest. But my eyes were sticky and they burned when I tried to close them.

It was that woman. It was the weaving of her form down the street, the flash of her white sickly face. The bed got intolerable. I turned on the light and lit a cigarette. It burned in my throat. I threw it away and resolved to give up smoking forever.

Once more in bed. And I tossed. That woman. How I loved her! The coil of her form, the hunger in her hunted eyes, the fur at her neck, the run in her hose, the feeling in my chest, the color of her coat, the flash of her face, the tingle in my fingers, the floating after her down the street, the coldness of the glittering stars, the dumb slither of a warm crescent moon, the taste of the match, the smell of the sea, the softness of the night, the stevedores, the click of poolballs, the beads of music, the coil of her form, the music of her heels, the stubbornness of her gait, the old man with a book, the woman, the woman, the woman.

I had an idea. I threw the covers off and leaped out of bed. What an idea! It came to me like an avalanche, like a house falling down, like the smash of glass. I felt on fire and crazy. There were papers and pencils in the drawer. I scooped them up and hurried to the kitchen. It was cold in the kitchen. I lit the oven and opened the oven door. Sitting naked I started to write.

Love Everlasting

or

The Woman A Man Loves

or

Omnia Vincit Amor

by

Arturo Gabriel Bandini

Three titles.

Marvelous! A superb start. Three titles, just like that!

Amazing! Incredible! A genius! A genius indeed!
And that name. Ah, it looked magnificent.
Arturo Gabriel Bandini.

A name to consider in the long roll of time immortal: A name for endless ages. Arturo Gabriel Bandini. An even better-sounding name than Dante Gabriel Rossetti. And he was an Italian too. He belonged to my race.

I wrote: "Arthur Banning, the multi-millionaire oil-dealer, tour de force, prima facie, petit maître, table d'hôte, and great lover of ravishing, beautiful, exotic, saccharine, and constellation-like women in all parts of the world, in every corner of the globe, women in Bombay, India, land of the Taj Mahal, of Gandhi and Buddha; women in Naples, land of Italian art and Italian fantasy; women in the Riviera; women at Lake Banff; women at Lake Louise; in the Swiss Alps; at the Ambassador Coconut Grove in Los Angeles, California; women at the famed Pons Asinorum in Europe; this same Arthur Banning, scion of an old Virginia family, land of George Washington and great American traditions; this same Arthur Banning, handsome and tall, six feet four inches in his sox, distingué, with teeth like pearls, and a certain, zippy, nippy, outré quality all women go for in a big way, this Arthur Banning, stood at the rail of his mighty, world-famous, much-loved, American, yacht, the Larchmont VIII, and watched with deleterious eyes, manly, virile, powerful, eyes, the carmine, red, beautiful, rays of Old Sol, better known as the sun, dip into the gloomy, phantasmagorically, black, waters of the Mediterranean Ocean, somewhere South of Europe, in the year of our Lord, nineteen hundred and thirty-five. And there he was, scion of a wealthy, famous, powerful, magniloquent, family, a gallant homo, with the world at his feet and the great, powerful, amazing, Banning, fortune at his disposal; and yet; as he stood there; something troubled Arthur Banning, tall, darkened, handsome, tanned, by the rays of Old Sol: and, what troubled him, was that, though he had traveled many lands and seas, and, rivers,

130

too, and though he made love, and, had love affairs, the whole world knew about, through the medium of the press, the powerful, grinding press, he, Arthur Banning, this scion, was unhappy, and though rich, famous, powerful, he was lonely and, incastellated for, love. And as he stood so incisively there on the deck of his Larchmont VIII, finest, most beautiful, most powerful, yacht, ever built, he wondered would the girl of his dreams, would he meet her soon, would she, the girl, of his dreams, be anything like the girl, of his boyhood dreams, back there when he was a boy, dreaming on the banks of the Potomac River, on his father's fabulous rich, wealthy, estate, or would she be poor?

"Arthur Banning lit his expensive, handsome, briar, pipe, and called to one of his underlings, a mere second mate, and, asked that underling for a match. That worthy, a famous, well-known, and, expert, character, in the world of ships, and the naval world, a man of international reputation, in the world of ships, and, sealing wax, did not impugn, but pro-offered the match with a respectful bow of obsequiousness, and, young Banning, handsome, tall, thanked him politely, albeit with a bit of gauche, and, then, resumed his quixotic dreaming about the fortunate girl who would some day be his bride and the woman of his wildest dreams.

"At that moment, a hushed moment, there was a sudden, stark, hideous, cry, from the hideous labyrinth of the briny sea, a cry that mingled with the flapping of the frigid waves against the prow of the proud, expensive, famous, Larchmont VIII, a cry of distress, a woman's cry! The cry of a woman! An appealing cry of bitter agony and deathlessness! A cry for help! Help! Help! With a quick glance at the storm-ridden waters, young Arthur Banning, went through an intense photosynthesis of regimentation, his keen, fine, handsome, blue, eyes looked away as he slipped off his costly evening jacket, a jacket which had cost $100, and he stood there in youthful splendor, his young, handsome, athletic, body, that had known gridiron struggles at Yale, and, soccer, at Oxford, in England, and like a Greek god it was silhouetted against the red rays of old sol, as it dipped into the waters of the blue Mediterranean. Help! Help! Help! Came that agonizing cry from a helpless woman, a poor, woman, half-naked, underfed, poverty-stricken, in cheap garments, as she felt that icy grip of stark, tragic, death, around her. Would she die without assistance? It was a crucible, and, sans ceremonie, and, defacto, the handsome Arthur Banning dove in."

I wrote that much at one fell swoop. It came to me so fast that I didn't get time to cross my t's or dot my i's. Now there was time for a breathing spell, and a chance to read it through. I did so.

Aha!

Wonderful stuff! Superb! I had never read anything like it before in my life. Amazing. I got up, spat on my hands, and rubbed them together.

Come on! Who wants to fight me? I'll fight every damned fool in this room. I can lick the whole world. It was like nothing on earth, that feeling. I was a ghost. I floated and soared and giggled and floated. This was too much. Who would have dreamed of it? That I should be able to write like this. My God! Amazing!

I went to the window and looked out. The fog was descending. Such a beautiful fog. See the beautiful fog. I tossed kisses into it. I stroked it with my hands. Dear Fog, you are a girl in a white dress and I am a spoon on the windowsill. It has been a hot day, and I am hot all over, so please kiss me, dear fog. I wanted to jump, to live, to die, to, to sleep wide awake in a dreamless dream. Such wonderful things. Such wonderful clarity. I was dying and the dead and the ever-living. I was the sky and not the sky. There was too much to say, and no way to say it.

Ah, see the stove. Who would have believed it! A stove. Imagine. Beautiful stove. Oh stove I love you. From now on I shall be faithful, pouring my love upon you every hour. Oh stove, hit me. Hit me in the eye. Oh stove, how beautiful is your hair. Let me pee in it, because I love you so madly, you honey, you immortal stove. And my hand. There it is. My hand. The hand that wrote. Lord, a hand. Such a hand too. The hand that wrote. Me and you and my hand and Keats. John Keats and Arturo Bandini and my hand, the hand of John Keats Bandini. Wonderful. Oh hand land band stand grand land.

Yes, I wrote it.

Ladies and gentlemen of the committee, of the titty committee, ditty, bitty, committee, I wrote it, ladies and gentlemen, I wrote it. Yes indeed. I will not deny it: a poor offering, if I may say so, a mere nothing. But thank you for your kind words. Yes, I love you all. Honestly. I love every one of you, peew, stew, meew, pheew. I love especially the ladies, the women, the wombmen. Let them disrobe and come forward. One at a time please. You there, you gorgeous blonde bitch. I shall have you first. Hurry please, my time is limited. I have much work to do. There is so little time. I am a writer, you know, my books you know, immortality you know, fame you know, you know fame, don't you, fame, you know him, don't you. Fame and all that, tut tut, a mere incident in the time of man. I merely sat down at that little table yonder. With a pencil, yes. A gift of God — no doubt about it. Yes, I believe in God. Of course. God. My dear friend God. Ah, thank you, thank you. The table? Of course. For the museum? Of course. No no. No need to charge admission. The children: admit them free, for nothing. I want all children to touch it. Oh thank you. Thank you. Yes, I accept the gift. Thank you, thank you all. Now I go to Europe and the Soviet Republics. The people of Europe await me. A wonderful people, those Europeans, wonderful. And the Russians, I love them, my friends, the Russians. Goodbye, goodbye. Yes, I love you all. My work, you know. So much of it: my opus, my books, my volumes. Goodbye goodbye.

I sat down and wrote again. The pencil crawled across the page. The page filled. I turned it over. The pencil moved down. Another page. Up one side and down the other. The pages mounted. Through the window came the fog, bashful and cool. Soon the room filled. I wrote on. Page eleven. Page twelve.

I looked up. It was daylight. Fog choked the room. The gas was out. My hands were numb. A blister showed on my pencil finger. My eyes burned. My back ached. I could barely move from the cold. But never in my life had I felt better.

TWENTY

That day at the cannery I was no good. I mashed my finger on the can dump. But thank God no harm was done. The hand that wrote was untouched. It was the other hand, the left hand; my left hand is no good anyway, cut it off if you like. At noon I fell asleep on the docks. When I awoke I was afraid to open my eyes. Was I blind? Had blindness stricken me so early in my career? But I opened my eyes, and thank God I could see. The afternoon moved like lava. Someone dropped a box and it hit me on the knee. It didn't matter. Any part of me gentlemen, but spare my eyes and my right hand.

At quitting time I hurried home. I took the bus. It was my only nickel. On the bus I fell asleep. It was the wrong bus. I had to walk five miles. Eating dinner, I wrote. A very bad dinner: hamburger. It's all right, Mama. Don't you dare fuss about me. I love hamburger. After dinner I wrote. Page twenty-three, page twenty-four. They were piling up. Midnight and I fell asleep in the kitchen. I rolled off the chair and cracked my head against the stove leg. Tut tut, old stove, forget it. My hand is all right, and so are my eyes; nothing else matters. Hit me again, if you like, right in the stomach. My mother pulled off my clothes and put me to bed.

Next night I wrote until dawn again. I got four hours sleep. That day I brought paper and pencil to work. On the bus going to the cannery a bee stung me on the nape of the neck. How absurd! A bee to sting the genius. You silly bee! Be on your way, if you please. You should be ashamed of yourself. Suppose you had stung me on the left hand? It's ridiculous. I fell asleep again on the bus. When I woke up the bus was at the end of the line, clear over on the San Pedro side of Los Angeles Harbor, six miles from the cannery. I took the ferry back. Then I took another bus. It was ten o'clock when I reached the cannery.

Shorty Naylor stood picking his teeth with a match.

"Well?"

"My mother's sick. They've taken her to the hospital."

"That's too bad," was all he said.

That morning I sneaked from work to the lavatory. I wrote in there. The flies were numberless. They hovered over me, crawled on my hands and on the paper. Very intelligent flies. No doubt they were reading what I wrote. Once I stood perfectly still so that they might crawl over the tablet and examine every word thoroughly. They were the loveliest flies I had ever known.

At noon I wrote in the cafe. It was crowded, smelling of grease and strong soup. I hardly noticed it. When the whistle blew I saw my plate before me. It hadn't been touched.

In the afternoon I sneaked back to the lavatory. I wrote in there for half an hour. Then Manuel came. I hid the tablet and pencil.

"The boss wants you."

I went to see the boss.

"Where the hell you been?"

"My mother. She's worse. I was using the telephone, calling the hospital."

He rubbed his face.

"That's too bad."

"It's pretty serious."

He clucked.

"Too bad. Will she pull through?"

"I doubt it. They say it's only a matter of moments."

"God. I'm sorry to hear that."

"She's been a swell mother to me. Perfect. I wouldn't know what to do if she passed on. I think I'd kill myself. She's the only friend I have in the world."

"What's the trouble?"

"Pulmonary thrombosis."

He whistled.

"God! That's awful."

"But that's not all."

"Not all?"

"Arteriosclerosis, too."

"Good God Almighty."

I felt the tears coming and sniffed. All at once I realized that what I had said about my mother being the only friend I had in the world was true. And I was sniffing because the whole thing was possible, with me, a poor kid, slaving my life away in this cannery; and my mother dying, and me, a poor kid without hope or money, slaving away hopelessly while my mother expired, her last thoughts of me, a poor kid, slaving away in a fish cannery. It was a heart-breaking thought. I was gushing tears.

"She's been wonderful," I said, sobbing. "Her whole life has been sacrificed for my success. It hurts me to the core."

"It's tough," Shorty said. "I think I know how you feel."

My head sank. I dragged myself away, tears streaming down my face. I was surprised that such a bare-faced lie could come so near breaking my heart.

"No. You don't understand. You *can't*! No one understands this thing I feel."

He hurried after me.

"Listen," he smiled. "Why don't you be sensible and take the day off? Go to the hospital! Stay with your mother! Cheer her up! Stay a few days—a week! It'll be all right here. I'll give you full time. I know how you feel. Hell, I guess I had a mother once."

I gritted my teeth and shook my head.

"No. I can't. I won't. My duty is here, with the rest of the fellows. I don't want you to play favorites. My mother would want it this way too. Even if she were drawing her last breath I know she would say so."

He grabbed my shoulders and shook me.

"No!" I said. "I won't do it."

"See here! Who's the boss? Now you do what I tell you. You get out of here and get up to that hospital, and stay there until your mother is better!"

At last I gave in, and reached for his hand.

"God, how wonderful you are! Thanks! God, I'll never forget this."

He patted my shoulder.

"Forget it. I understand these things. I guess I had a mother once."

From his wallet he drew a picture.

"Look," he smiled.

I held the faded photograph to my blurred eyes. She was a square, bricky woman in a bridal gown that fell like sheets out of the sky, tumbling at her feet. Behind her was an imitation background, trees and bushes, apple blossoms, and roses in full bloom, the canvas scenery slit with holes plain to see.

"My mother," he said. "That picture's fifty years old."

I thought she was the ugliest woman I ever saw. Her jaw was as square as a policeman's. The flowers in her hand, held like a potato-masher, were wilted. Her veil was crooked, like a veil hanging from a broken curtain rod. The edges of her mouth were hooked upward in an unusually cynical smile. She looked as though she despised the idea of being all dressed up to marry one of those damned Naylors.

"It's beautiful — too beautiful for words."

"She was a wonder all right."

"She looks it. There's something soft about her — like a hill in the twilight, like a cloud in the distance, something sweet and spiritual; you know what I mean — my metaphors are inadequate."

"Yeah. She died of pneumonia."

"God," I said. "To think of it! A wonderful woman like that! The limitations of so-called science! And it all started from a common cold, too, didn't it?"

"Yeah. That's what happened all right."

"We moderns! What fools we are! We forget the unearthly beauty of the old things, the precious things — like that picture. God, she's marvelous."

"Yeah. God, God."

TWENTY-ONE

That afternoon I wrote on a picnic bench in the park. The sun slid away and darkness crept from the east. I wrote in the half-light. When the damp wind rose out of the sea I quit and walked home. Mona and my mother knew nothing, thinking I was arriving from the cannery.

After supper I began again. It wasn't going to be a short story after all. I counted thirty-three thousand, five hundred and sixty words, not including a's and an's. A novel, a full novel. There were two hundred and twenty-four paragraphs, and three thousand five hundred and eighty sentences. One sentence contained four hundred and thirty-eight words, the longest sentence I had ever seen. I was proud of it and I knew it would stupefy the critics. After all, not everybody could get them off at that length.

And I wrote on, whenever I could, a line or two in the mornings, all day at the park for three days, and pages at night.

The days and nights passed under the pencil like the running feet of children. Three tablets were packed with writing, and then a fourth. A week later it was finished. Five tablets. 69,009 words.

It was the story of the passionate loves of Arthur Banning. In his yacht he went from country to country seeking the woman of his dreams. He had love affairs with women from every race and country in the world. I went to the dictionary for all my countries, and there was none I missed. There were sixty of them, and a passionate love affair in each.

But Arthur Banning never found the woman of his dreams.

At exactly 3:27 a.m. on Friday, August 7th, I finished the story. The last word of the last page was exactly what I wished.

It was "Death."

My hero shot himself through the head.

He held a gun to his temple and spoke.

"I have failed to find the woman of my dreams," he said. "Now I am ready for Death. Ah, sweet mystery of Death."

I didn't exactly write that he pulled the trigger. This was illustrated by suggestion, which proved my ability to use restraint in a smashing climax.

And so it was finished.

TWENTY-TWO

When I reached home the next evening Mona was reading the manuscript. The tablets were piled on the table, and she was reading the final words on the last page, with its terrific climax. She seemed wild-eyed with intense interest. I pulled off my jacket and rubbed my hands together.

"Ha!" I said "I see you're absorbed. Gripping, isn't it?"

She looked up with a sickly face.

"It's silly," she said. "Plain silly. It doesn't grip me. It gripes me."

"Oh," I said. "Is that so!"

I walked across the room.

"And just who the hell do you think you are?"

"It's silly. I had to laugh. I skipped most of it. I didn't even read three tablets of it."

I shook my fist in front of her nose.

"And how would you like me to smash your face into a bloody, drooling pulp?"

"It's smart-alecky. All those big words!"

I tore the tablets from her.

"You Catholic ignoramus! You filthy Comstock! You disgusting, nauseating, clod-hopping celibate!"

My spittle sprinkled her face and hair. Her handkerchief moved across her neck and she pushed me out of the way. She smiled.

"Why didn't your hero kill himself on the first page instead of the last? It would have made a lot better story."

I got her by the throat.

"Be very careful, what you say, you Roman harlot. I warn you — be very very very careful."

She tore herself loose, clawing my arm.

"It's the worst book I ever read."

I grabbed her again. She jumped from the chair and fought wildly, clawing at my face with her nails. I backed away, shouting at every step.

"You sanctimonious, retch-provoking she-nun of a bitch-infested nausea-provoking nun of a vile boobish baboon of a brummagem Catholic heritage."

On the table was a vase. She spied it, walked to the table and picked it up. She played with it in her hands, stroking it, smiling, feeling its weight, then smiling at me threateningly. Then she poised it at her shoulder, ready to heave it at my head.

"Ha!" I said. "That's right! Throw it!"

I stripped my shirt open, buttons flying everywhere, and

stuck out my bare chest. I jumped down on my knees before her, my chest jutting out. I beat my chest, hammered it with both fists until it turned red and stung.

"Strike!" I shouted. "Let me have it! Renew the Inquisition. Kill me! Commit fratricide. Let these floors run red with the rich, pure blood of a genius who dared!"

"You fool. You can't write. You can't write at all."

"You slut! You nunny slutty slut out of the belly of the Roman Harlot."

She smiled bitterly.

"Call me anything you like. But keep your hands off me."

"Put that vase down."

She considered a moment, shrugged, and put it down. I got up from my knees. We ignored one another. It was as if nothing had happened. She went over the rug, picking up the buttons from my shirt. For a while I sat about, doing nothing but sitting and thinking of what she had said about the book. She walked into the bedroom. I could hear the swish of a comb passing through her hair.

"What was the matter with the story?" I asked.

"It's silly. I didn't like it."

"Why not?"

"Because it was silly."

"Damn it! Criticize it! Don't say it was silly! Criticize it! What's wrong with it? Why is it silly?"

She came to the door.

"Because it's silly. That's all I can say about it."

I rushed her to the wall. I was furious. I pinned her arms against her, locked her firmly with my legs, and glared her in the face. She was speechless with anger. Her teeth chattered helplessly, her face whitened and became blotchy. But now that I had her, I was afraid to let her go. I had not forgotten the butcher knife.

"It's the craziest book I ever read!" she screamed. "The

awfullest, the vilest, craziest, funniest book in the world! It was
so bad I couldn't even read it."

I decided to be indifferent. I released her and snapped my
fingers under her nose.

"Phooey! That for you. Your opinion doesn't bother me
in the least."

I walked to the middle of the room. I stood there and spoke
to the walls at large.

"They can't touch us. No—they can't! We have put
the Church to rout. Dante, Copernicus, Galileo, and now
me—Arturo Bandini, son of a humble carpenter. We go on and
on. We are above them. We even transcend their ridiculous
heaven."

She rubbed her bruised arms. I walked over to her and
raised my hand to the ceiling.

"They can gibbet us, and burn us, but we go on—we—
the yea-sayers; the outcasts; the eternal ones; the yea-sayers to
the end of time."

Before I could duck she picked up the vase and threw it.
Her aim was perfect at such close range. The vase hit me just
as I turned my head. It struck me behind the ear and smashed
to pieces. For a moment I thought my skull was fractured. But
it was a small, thin vase. I felt in vain for blood. It had shattered
without even scratching me. The tinkling pieces scattered about
the room. Not one trace of blood, and scarcely a hair out of place
on my head.

A miracle!

Calm and unhurt I turned around. With my finger to the
ceiling like one of the Apostles I spoke.

"Even God Almighty is on our side. For amen I say unto
you, even when they breaketh vases over our heads, they hurteth
us not, neither do our heads cracketh open."

She was glad I was unhurt. Laughing, she went into the
bedroom. She lay on the bed and I heard her laughing and

laughing. I stood at the door and watched her twisting a pillow with delight.

"Laugh," I said. "Go ahead. For amen I say unto you, he that laugheth last laugheth best, and ye must say aye, aye again and again, thus spake Zarathustra."

TWENTY-THREE

My mother came home, her arms wrapped around packages. I jumped from the divan and followed her into the kitchen. She put the packages down and faced me. She was out of breath, her face red from pounding blood, for the stairs were always too much for her.

"Did you read the story?"

"Yes," she gasped. "I certainly did."

I took her by the shoulders, gripping them hard.

"It was a great story—wasn't it? Answer quick!"

She clasped her hands, swayed, and closed her eyes.

"It certainly was!"

I didn't believe her.

"Don't lie to me, please. You know perfectly well I hate all forms of pretense. I'm not brummagem. I always want the truth."

Mona got up then, and came and stood inside the door. She leaned with her hands behind her and smiled the smile of Mona Lisa.

"Tell that to Mona," I said.

My mother turned to Mona.

"I read it—didn't I, Mona?"

Mona's expression was unchanged.

"See!" my mother said in triumph. "Mona *knows* I read it, don't you Mona?"

She turned to Mona again.

"I said I liked it, didn't I Mona?"

Mona's face was exactly the same.

"See! Mona knows I liked it — don't you Mona?"

I started beating my chest.

"Good God!" I yelled. "Talk to me! Me! Me! Me! Not Mona! Me! Me! Me!"

My mother's hands went up in despair. She was under some sort of tension. She was not all sure of herself.

"But I just *told* you I thought it was wonderful!"

"Don't lie to me. No chicanery allowed."

She sighed and resolutely said it again.

"It's wonderful. For the third time I say it's wonderful. Wonderful."

"Stop lying."

Her eyes tumbled and tossed. She wanted to scream, to cry. She pressed her temples and tried to think of some other way to say it.

"Then what do you *want* me to say?"

"I want the truth, if you please. Only the truth."

"All right then. The truth is, it's wonderful."

"Stop lying. The least I can expect from the woman who gave me life is some semblance of the truth."

She pressed my hand and put her face next to mine.

"Arturo," she pleaded. "I swear I like it. I swear."

She meant that.

Now here was something at last. Here was a woman who understood me. Here before me, this woman, my mother. She understood me. Blood of my blood, bone of my bone, she could appreciate my prose. She could stand before the world and pronounce it wonderful. Here was a woman for the ages, and a woman who was an aesthete for all her homely ways, a critic by intuition. Something within me softened.

"Little mother," I whispered. "Dear little mother. Dear

sweet darling mother. I love you so much. Life is so hard for you, my dear darling mother."

I kissed her, tasting the salty texture of her neck. She seemed so tired, so over-worked. Where was justice in this world, that this woman should suffer without complaint? Was there a God in heaven who judged and found her his own? There should be! There must be!

"Dear little mother. I'm going to dedicate my book to you. To you—my mother. To my mother, in grateful appreciation. To my mother, without whom this great work would have been impossible. To my mother, in grateful appreciation by a son who shall not forget."

With a shriek Mona turned and went back to the bedroom.

"Laugh!" I yelled. "Laugh! You jackass!"

"Dear little mother," I said. "Dear little mother."

"Laugh!" I said. "You intense moron! Laugh!"

"Dear little mother. For you: my mother: a kiss!"

And I kissed her.

"The hero made me think of you," she smiled.

"Dear little mother."

She coughed, hesitated. Something was disturbing her. She was trying to say something.

"The only thing is, does your hero have to make love to that Negro woman? That woman in South Africa?"

I laughed and hugged her. This was amusing indeed. I kissed her and patted her cheek. Ho ho, like a little child she was, like a wee bit of a baby.

"Dear little mother. I see the writing made a profound effect upon you. It stirred you to the very brink of your pure soul, dear little mother of mine. Ho, ho."

"I didn't like that Chinese girl business, either."

"Dear little mother. My little baby mother."

"And I didn't like that business with the Eskimo woman. I thought it was awful. It disgusted me."

I shook my finger at her.

"Now, now. Let us eliminate Puritanism here. Let us have no prudery. Let us try to be logical and philosophical."

She bit her lip and frowned. There was something else biting inside that head of hers. She thought a moment, then looked simply into my eyes. I knew the trouble: she was afraid to mention it, whatever it was.

"Well," I said. "Speak. Out with it. What else?"

"The place he slept with the chorus girls. I didn't like that either. Twenty chorus girls! I thought that was terrible. I didn't like it at all."

"Why not?"

"I don't think he ought to sleep with so many women."

"Oh you don't eh? And why not?"

"I just don't—that's all."

"Why not? Don't beat about the bush. Speak your opinion, if you have any. Otherwise, shut up. You women!"

"He should find a nice clean little Catholic girl, and settle down and marry her."

So that was it! At last the truth was out. I seized her by the shoulders and spun her around until my face was next to hers, my eyes on a level with hers.

"Look at me," I said. "You profess to be my mother. Well, look at me! Do I look like a person who would sell his soul for mere pelf? Do you think I give a hang for mere public opinion? Answer that!"

She backed away.

I pounded my chest.

"Answer me! Don't stand there like a woman, like an idiot, a bourgeois Catholic Comstocking smut-hound. I demand an answer!"

Now she became defiant.

"The hero was nasty. He committed adultery on almost every page. Women, women, women! He was impure from the beginning. He turned my stomach."

"Ha!" I said. "At last it is out! At last the awful truth emerges! Papism returns! The Catholic mind again! The Pope of Rome waves his lewd banner."

I walked into the living room and addressed the door.

"There you have it all. The riddle of the Universe. The transvaluation of values already transvaluated. Romanism. Red Neckery. Papism. The Roman Harlot in all her gaudy horror! Vaticism. Aye — verily I say unto you that unless ye become yea-sayers ye shall become one of the damned! Thus spake Zarathustra!"

TWENTY-FOUR

After supper I brought the manuscript into the kitchen. I spread the tablets on the table and lit a cigarette.

"Now we'll see how silly it is."

As I began to read I heard Mona singing.

"Silence!"

I settled myself and read the first ten lines. When I was finished with that much I dropped the book like a dead snake and got up from the table. I walked around the kitchen. Impossible! It couldn't be true!

"Something's wrong here. It's too hot here. It doesn't suit me. I need room, plenty of fresh air."

I opened the window and looked out for a moment. Behind me lay the book. Well — go back and read it, Bandini. Don't stand at the window. The book isn't here; it's back there, behind you, on the table. Go back and read it.

Closing my mouth tightly I sat down and read another five lines. The blood rushed to my face. My heart plowed like a wheel.

"This is strange; very strange indeed."

From the living room came Mona's voice. She was singing. A hymn. Lord, a hymn at a time like this. I opened the door
and put out my head.

"Stop that singing or I'll show you something really silly."

"I'll sing if I feel like it."

"No hymns. I forbid hymns."

"And I'll sing hymns too."

"Sing a hymn—and die. Suit yourself."

"Who died?" my mother said.

"Nobody," I said. "Nobody—yet."

I returned to the book. Another ten lines. I jumped up
and bit my nails. I tore the cuticle loose on my thumb. The pain
flashed. Closing my eyes, I seized the loose cuticle between my
teeth and ripped it off. A tiny spot of red blood appeared under
the nail.

"Bleed! Bleed to death!"

My clothes stuck to me. I hated that kitchen. At the window I watched the stream of traffic down Avalon Boulevard.
Never had I heard such noise. Never had I felt such pain as in
my thumb. Pain and noise. All the horns in the world were out
in that street. The clamor was driving me crazy. I couldn't live
in a place like this and write. Downstairs came the zzzzzzzzz of
a bath-spigot. Who was taking a bath at this hour? What fiend?
Maybe the plumbing was out of order. I ran through the apartment to our bathroom and flushed the water. It worked all
right—but it was noisy, so noisy I wondered that I had never
noticed it before.

"What's the matter?" my mother said.

"There's too much noise around here. I can't create in this
racket. I tell you I'm getting tired of this madhouse."

"I think it's very quiet tonight."

"Don't contradict me—you woman."

I went back to the kitchen. This was an impossible place
to write. No wonder. No wonder—what? Well, no wonder it was

an impossible place to write. No wonder? What are you talking about? No wonder — *what*? This kitchen was a detriment. This neighborhood was a detriment. This town was a detriment. I sucked the pounding thumb wound. The pain was tearing me to pieces. I heard my mother speak to Mona.

"What's the matter with him now?"

"He's foolish," Mona said.

I rushed into the room.

"I heard you!" I screamed. "And I warn you to shut up! I'll show you who's silly around here."

"I didn't say *you* were silly," Mona said. "I said your story was silly. Not you." She smiled. "I said *you* were foolish. It was your book that I said was silly."

"Be careful! As God is my judge, I warn you."

"What's the matter with you two?" my mother said.

"She knows," I said. "Ask her."

Steeling myself for the ordeal, I gritted my teeth and returned to the book. I held the page before me, and kept my eyes closed. I was afraid to read the lines. No writing could be done in this asylum. No art could come from this chaos of stupidity. Beautiful prose demanded quiet, peaceful surroundings. Perhaps even soft music. No wonder! No wonder!

I opened my eyes and tried to read it. No good. It didn't work. I couldn't read it. I tried it out loud. No good. This book was no good. It was somewhat verbose; there were too many words in it. It was somewhat stodgy. It was a very good book. It missed. It was quite bad. It was worse than that. It was a lousy book. It was a stinking book. It was the goddamnedest book I ever saw. It was ridiculous; it was funny; it was silly; oh it's silly, silly, silly, silly, silly. Shame on you, you silly old thing, for writing a silly thing like this. Mona is right. It's silly.

It's on account of the women. They have poisoned my mind. I can feel it coming — stark madness. The writing of a maniac. Insanity. Ha! Look! He's a madman! Look at him! One of the Jukes! Stark, raving mad. He got that way from too many secret women, sir. I feel awfully sorry for him. A pathetic case, sir. Once he was a good Catholic kid. He went to church and all that sort of thing. Was very devoted, sir. A model boy. Educated by the nuns, a fine young chap once. Now a pathetic case, sir. Very touching. Suddenly he changed. Yeah. Something happened to the guy. He started off on the wrong foot after his old man died, and look what happened.

He got ideas. He had all those phony women. There was always something just a bit screwy about the guy, but it took those phonies to bring it out. I used to see the kid around here, walking around by himself. He lived with his mother and sister in that stucco house across from the school. He used to come into Jim's Place a lot. Ask Jim about him. Jim knew him well. Worked at the cannery. Had a lot of jobs around here. Couldn't keep any though — too erratic. A screw loose, a nut. Nuts, I tell you, plain nuts. Yeah — too many women, the wrong kind. You should have heard the monkey talk. Like a lunatic. Goddamnedest liar in Los Angeles County. Had hallucinations. Delusions of grandeur. Menace to society. Followed women in the streets. Used to get mad at flies and eat them. Women did it. Killed a lot of crabs too. Killed them all afternoon. Just plain screwy. Screwiest guy in Los Angeles County. Glad they locked him up. You say they found him wandering around the docks in a stupor? Well — that's him. Probably looking for more crabs to kill. Dangerous, I tell you. Belongs behind the bars. Ought to look into it very careful. Keep him there the rest of his life. Feel safer with the lunatic in the bug house where he belongs. A sad case though. Awful sorry for his mother and sister. They pray for him every night. Can you imagine that? Yeah! Maybe they're crazy too.

I threw myself across the table and started to cry. I wanted to pray again. Like nothing else in the world I wanted to say prayers.

Ha! The madman wants to pray!

A praying madman! Maybe it's his religious background. Maybe he was too pious when a kid. Funny thing about the guy. Very funny. I bit my knuckles. I clawed the table. My teeth found the flashing thumb cuticle. I gnawed. The tablets lay all about me on the table. What a writer! A book on California Fisheries! A book on California puke!

Laughter.

In the next room I heard them, my mother and Mona. They were talking about money. My mother was complaining bitterly. She was saying that we would never catch up on my salary at the fish-cannery. She was saying we would all go to live at Uncle Frank's house. He would take good care of us. I knew the origin of that kind of talk. Uncle Frank's words. He had been speaking to my mother again. I knew. And I knew she wasn't repeating all he had really said: that I was worthless and couldn't be depended on, that she should always expect the worst from me. And my mother was doing all the talking, with Mona not answering. Why didn't Mona answer her? Why did Mona have to be so rude? So callous?

I jumped up and walked in.

"Answer your mother when she addresses you!"

The instant Mona saw me she was terrified. It was the first time I ever saw that look of fright in her eyes. I sprang into action. It was what I had always wanted. I moved in on her.

She said, "Be careful!"

She was holding her breath, pressing herself against the chair.

"Arturo!" my mother said.

Mona stepped into the bedroom and slammed the door. She held her weight against the other side. She called to my mother to keep me away. With a lunge I pushed the door open. Mona backed to the bed, tumbled backwards upon it. She was panting.

"Be careful!"

"You nun!"

"Arturo!" my mother said.

"You nun! So it was silly, was it? So it made you laugh, did it? So it was the worst book you ever read, was it?"

I lifted my fist and let fly. It struck her in the mouth. She held her lips and dropped into the pillows. My mother came screaming. Blood oozed through Mona's fingers.

"So you laughed at it, did you? You sneered! At the work of a genius. You! At Arturo Bandini! Now Bandini strikes back. He strikes in the name of liberty!"

My mother covered her with her arms and body. I tried to pull my mother away. She tore at me like a cat.

"Get out!" she said.

I grabbed my jacket and left. Back there my mother was babbling. Mona was moaning. The feeling was that I would never see them again. And I was glad.

TWENTY-FIVE

In the street I didn't know where to go. The town had two worthwhile directions: East and West. East lay Los Angeles. West for a half-mile lay the sea. I walked in the direction of the sea. It was bitterly cold that summer night. The fog had begun to blow in. A wind pushed it this way and that, great streaks of crawling white. In the channel I heard foghorns mooing like a carload of steers. I lit a cigarette. There was blood on my knuckles—Mona's. I wiped it on the leg of my pants. It didn't come off. I held up my fist and let the fog wet it with a cold kiss. Then I wiped it again. But it didn't come off. Then I rubbed my knuckles in the dirt at the sidewalk's edge until the blood disappeared, but I tore the skin on my knuckles doing it, and now my blood was flowing.

"Good. Bleed—you. Bleed!"

I crossed the schoolyard and walked down Avalon, walking fast. Where are you going, Arturo? The cigarette was hateful,
like a mouthful of hair. I spat it out ahead of me, then crushed
it carefully with my heel. Over my shoulder I looked at it. I was
amazed. It still burned, faint smoke curling in the fog. I walked
a block, thinking about that cigarette. It still lived. It hurt me
that it still burned. Why should it still burn? Why hadn't it gone
out? An evil omen, perhaps. Why should I deny that cigarette
entry into the world of cigarette spirits? Why let it burn and suffer
so miserably? Had I come to this? Was I so terrible a monster
as to deny that cigarette its rightful demise?

I hurried back.

There it lay.

I crushed it to a brown mass.

"Goodbye, dear cigarette. We shall meet again in paradise."

Then I walked on. The fog licked me with its many cold
tongues. I buttoned up my leather jacket, all but the last button.

Why not button the last one too?

This annoyed me. Should I button it, or should I leave
it unbuttoned, the laughingstock of the button world, a useless
button?

I will leave it unbuttoned.

No, I will button it.

Yes, I will unbutton it.

I did neither. Instead I invoked a master decision. I tore
the button off my collar and threw it into the street.

"I'm sorry, button. We have been friends a long time. Often
I have touched you with my fingers, and you have kept me warm
on cold nights. Forgive me for what I have done. We too shall
meet in paradise."

At the bank I stopped and saw the match scratches on
the wall. The Limbo of match scratches, their punishing ground
for being without souls. Only one match scratch here had
a soul — only one, the scratch made by the woman in the

purple coat. Should I stop and visit it? Or should I go on?
I will stop.
No, I'll go on.
Yes I will.
No I won't.
Yes and no.
Yes and no.
I stopped.

I found the match scratch she had made, the woman in the purple coat. How beautiful it was! What artistry in that scratch! What expression! I lit a match, a long heavy scratch. Then I forced the burning sulphur tip into the scratch she had made. It clung to the wall, sticking out.

"I am seducing you. I love you, and publicly I am giving you my love. How fortunate you are!"

It clung there, over her artistic mark. Then it fell, the burning sulphur growing cold. I walked on, taking mighty military steps, a conqueror who had ravished the rare soul of a match scratch.

But why had the match grown cold and fallen? It bothered me. I was panic stricken. Why had this happened? What had I done to deserve this? I was Bandini — the writer. Why had the match failed me?

I hurried back in anger. I found the match where it had fallen on the sidewalk, lying there cold and dead for all the world to see. I picked it up.

"Why did you fall? Why do you forsake me in my hour of triumph? I am Arturo Bandini — the mighty writer. What have you done to me?"

No answer.

"Speak! I demand an explanation."

No answer.

"Very well. I have no other choice. I must destroy you."

I snapped it in two and dropped it in the gutter. It landed

near another match, one that was unbroken, a very handsome match with a dash of blue sulphur around its neck, a very worldly and sophisticated match. And there lay mine, humiliated, with a broken spine.

"You embarrass me. Now shall you really suffer. I leave you to the laughter of the match kingdom. Now all the matches will see you and make sneering remarks. So be it. Bandini speaks. Bandini, mighty master of the pen."

But a half block away it seemed terribly unfair. That poor match! That pathetic fellow! This was all so unnecessary. He had done his very best. I knew how badly he felt. I went back and got him. I put him to my mouth and chewed him to a pulp.

Now all the other matches would find him unrecognizable. I spat him out in my hand. There he lay, broken and mashed, already in a state of decomposition. Fine! Wonderful! A miracle of decline. Bandini, I congratulate you! You have performed a miracle here. You have sped up the eternal laws and hurried the return to the source. Good for you, Bandini! Wonderful work. Potent. A veritable god, a mighty superman; a master of life and letters.

I passed the Acme Poolhall, nearing the secondhand store. Tonight the store was open. The window was the same as that night three weeks ago, when she had peered into it, the woman with the purple coat. And there it was, the sign: Highest Prices Paid For Old Gold.

All of this from that night of so long ago, when I'd defeated Gooch in the half-mile and won so gloriously for America. And where was Gooch now, Sylvester Gooch, that mighty Dutchman? Dear old Gooch! Not soon would he forget Bandini. A great runner he was, almost equal to Bandini. What tales he would have for his grandchildren! When we met again in some other land we would talk of old times, Gooch and I. But where was he now, that streak of Dutch lightning? Doubtless back in Holland, tinkering with his windmills and tulips and wooden shoes, that mighty man, almost the equal of Bandini, waiting for death among sweet memories, waiting for Bandini.

But where was she — my woman of that bright night? Ah fog, lead me to her. I have much to forget. Make me like unto you, floating water, misty as the soul, and carry me to the arms of the woman with the white face. Highest Prices Paid For Old Gold. Those words had gone deep into her eyes, deep into her nerves, deep into her brain, far into the blackness of her brain behind that white face. They had made a gash back there, a match streak of memory, a flare she would carry to the grave, an impression. Wonderful, wonderful, Bandini, how profoundly you see! How mysterious is your nearness to godliness. Such words, lovely words, beauty of language, deep in the temple of her mind.

And I see you now, you woman of that night — I see you in the sanctity of some dirty harbor bedroom flop-joint, with the mist outside, and you lying with legs loose and cold from the fog's lethal kisses, and hair smelling of blood, sweet as blood, your frayed and ripped hose hanging from a rickety chair beneath the cold yellow light of a single, spotted bulb, the odor of dust and wet leather spinning about, your tattered blue shoes tumbled sadly at the bedside, your face lined with the tiring misery of Woolworth defloration and exhausting poverty, your lips slutty, yet soft blue lips of beauty calling me to come come come to that miserable room and feast myself upon the decaying rapture of your form, that I might give you a twisting beauty for misery and a twisting beauty for cheapness, my beauty for yours, the light becoming blackness as we scream, our miserable love and farewell to the tortuous flickering of a grey dawn that refused to really begin and would never really have an ending.

Highest Prices Paid For Old Gold.

An idea! The solution to all my problems. The escape of Arturo Bandini.

I entered.

"How late do you stay open?"

The Jew did not look up from his accounts behind the wire.
"Another hour."

"I'll be back."

When I got home they were gone. There was an unsigned note on the table. My mother had written it.

"We have gone to Uncle Frank's for the night. Come right over."

The bed coverlet had been stripped off, as well as one pillow case. They lay in a heap on the floor, dotted with blood. On the dresser were bandages and a blue bottle of disinfectant. A pan of water tinted red sat on the chair. Beside it lay my mother's ring. I put it in my pocket.

From under the bed I dragged the trunk. It contained many things, souvenirs of our childhood which my mother had carefully saved. One by one I lifted them out. A sentimental farewell, a look at past things before flight by Bandini. The lock of blonde hair in the tiny white prayer book: it was my hair as a child; the prayer book was a gift on the day of my First Communion.

Clippings from the San Pedro paper when I graduated from grade school; other clippings when I left high school. Clippings about Mona. A newspaper picture of Mona in her First Communion dress. Her picture and mine on Confirmation Day. Our picture on Easter Sunday. Our picture when we both sang in the choir. Our picture together on the Feast of the Immaculate Conception. A sheet of words from a spelling match when I was in grade school; 100% over my name.

Clippings about school plays. All of my report cards from the beginning. All of Mona's. I wasn't smart, but I always passed. Here was one: Arithmetic 70; History 80; Geography 70; Spelling 80; Religion 99; English 97. Never any trouble with religion or English for Arturo Bandini. And here was one of Mona's: Arithmetic 96; History 95; Geography 97; Spelling 94; Religion 90; English 90.

She could beat me at other things, but never at English

or religion. Ho! Very amusing, this. A great piece of anecdote for the biographers of Arturo Bandini. God's worst enemy making higher marks in religion than God's best friend, and both in the same family. A great irony. What a biography that would be! Ah Lord, to be alive and read it!

At the bottom of the trunk I found what I wanted. They were family jewels wrapped in a paisley shawl. Two solid gold rings, a solid gold watch and chain, a set of gold cuff links, a set of gold earrings, a gold brooch, a few gold pins, a gold cameo, a gold chain, little odds and ends of gold—jewels my father had bought during his lifetime.

"How much?" I said.

The Jew made a sour face.

"All junk. I can't sell it."

"How much though? What about that sign: Highest Prices Paid For Old Gold?"

"Maybe a hundred dollars, but I can't use it. Not much gold in it. Mostly plate."

"Give me two hundred and you can have all of it."

He smiled bitterly, his black eyes pinched between froggy lids.

"Never. Not in a million years."

"Make it a hundred and seventy-five."

He pushed the jewels toward me.

"Take it away. Not a cent more than fifty dollars."

"Make it a hundred and seventy-five."

We settled for a hundred and ten. One by one he handed me the bills. It was more money than I ever had in my life. I thought I would collapse from the sight of it. But I didn't let him know.

"It's piracy," I said. "You're robbing me."

"You mean charity. I'm practically giving you fifty dollars."

"Monstrous," I said. "Outrageous."

Five minutes later I was up the street at Jim's Place. He

was polishing glasses behind the counter. His greeting was always the same.

"Hello! And how's the cannery job?"

I seated myself, pulled out the roll of bills, and counted them again.

"Quite a roll you got there," he smiled.

"How much do I owe you?"

"Why — nothing."

"Are you sure?"

"But you don't owe me a cent."

"I'm leaving town," I said. "Back to headquarters. I thought I owed you a few dollars. I'm paying off all my debts."

He grinned at the money.

"I wish you owed me about half of that money."

"It's not all mine. Some of it belongs to the party. Expense money for traveling."

"Oh. Having a farewell party, eh?"

"Not that kind of a party. I mean, the Communist Party."

"You mean Russians?"

"Call it that if you like. Commissar Demetriev sent it. Expense money."

His eyes got bigger. He whistled and put down his towel.

"You a Communist?" He pronounced it with the wrong accent, so that it rhymed with Tunis.

I got up and went to the door and looked carefully up and down the street. Returning I nodded toward the rear of the store.

I whispered, "Anybody back there?"

He shook his head. I sat down. We stared at one another in silence. I wet my lips. He looked toward the street and back at me again. His eyes were bugging in and out. I cleared my throat.

"Can you keep your mouth shut? You look like a man I can trust. Can you?"

He swallowed hard, and leaned forward.

"Keep it quiet," I said. "Yes. I am a Communist."

"A Russian?"

"In principle — yes. Give me a chocolate malted."

It was like a stiletto jabbed in his ribs. He was afraid to take his eyes away. Even when he turned to put the drink in the mixer he looked over his shoulder. I chuckled and lit a cigarette.

"We're quite harmless," I laughed. "Yes quite."

He didn't say a word.

I drank the malt slowly, pausing now and then to chuckle. A gay little fearless laugh floated from my throat.

"But really! We're quite human. Quite!"

He watched me like a bank robber.

I laughed again, gaily, trilling, easily.

"Demetriev shall hear of this. In my next report I shall tell of it. Old Demetriev will roar in his black beard. How he'll roar, that black Russian wolf! But really — we're quite harmless — quite. I assure you, quite. But really, Jim. Didn't you know? But really —"

"No I didn't."

I trilled again.

"But surely! But certainly you must have known!"

I got up and laughed very humanly.

"Aye — old Demetriev shall hear of this. And how he'll roar in his black beard, that black Russian wolf!"

I stood in front of the magazine stand.

"And what is the bourgeoisie reading tonight?"

He said nothing. His bitter hostility stretched like a taut wire between us, and he polished glasses in a fury, one after another.

"You owe me for the drink," he said.

I gave him a ten dollar bill.

The cash register clanged. He drew out the change and smashed it down on the counter.

"Here you are! Anything else?"

I took all but a quarter. That was my usual tip.

"You forgot a quarter," he said

"Oh no!" I smiled. "That's for you — a tip."

"Don't want it. Keep your money."

Without a word, only smiling confidently, reminiscently, I put it into my pocket.

"Old Demetriev — how he'll roar, that black wolf."

"Do you want anything else?"

I took all five issues of *Artists and Models* from his shelf. The moment I touched them I knew why I had come to Jim's Place with so much money in my pocket.

"These, I'll take these."

He leaned over the counter.

"How many have you got there?"

"Five."

"I can only sell you two. The others are promised to somebody else."

I knew he was lying.

"Then two it is, Comrade."

As I stepped into the street his eyes bored into my back. I crossed the schoolyard. The windows in our apartment were unlighted. Ah, the women again. Here comes Bandini with his women. They were to be with me on my very last night in this town. All at once I felt the old hatefulness.

No. Bandini will not succumb. Never again!

I wadded the magazines and threw them away. They landed on the sidewalk, flapping in the fog, the dark photographs standing out like black flowers. I went for them and stopped. No, Bandini! A superman does not weaken. The strong man allows temptation at his elbow so he can resist it. Then I started for them once more. Courage, Bandini! Fight to the last ditch! With all my strength I wheeled away from the magazines and walked straight ahead toward the apartment. At the door

I looked back. They were invisible in the fog.

Sad legs lifted me up the creaking stairs. I opened the door and snapped the light on. I was alone. The solitude caressed, inflamed. No. Not this last night. For tonight I depart like a conqueror.

I lay down. Jumped up. Lay down. Jumped up. I walked around, searching. In the kitchen, in the bedroom. The clothes closet. I went to the door and smiled. I walked to the desk, to the window. In the fog the women flapped. In the room I searched. This is your last battle. You're winning. Keep on fighting.

But now I was walking to the door. And down the stairs. You're losing; fight like a superman! The grumbling fog gulped me. Not tonight, Bandini. Be not like dumb, driven cattle. Be a hero in the strife!

And yet I was on my way back, the magazine in my fist. So there he creeps — that weakling. Again he has fallen.

See him slinking through the fog with his bloodless women. Always he will slink through life with the bloodless women of papers and books. When it ends they will find him, as yet in that land of white dreams, groping in the fog of himself.

A tragedy, sir. A great tragedy. A boneless fluid existence, sir. And the body, sir. We found it down by the waterfront. Yes, sir. A bullet through the heart, sir. Yes, a suicide, sir. And what shall we do with the body, sir? For Science — a very good idea, sir. The Rockefeller Institute, no less. He would have wanted it that way, sir. His last earthly wish. A great lover of Science he was, sir — of Science and bloodless women.

I sat on the divan and turned the pages. Ah, the women, the women.

Suddenly I snapped my fingers.

Idea!

I threw down the magazines and raced about looking for a pencil. A novel! A brand new novel! What an idea! Holy God, what an idea! The first one failed, of course. But not this. *Here* was an idea! In this new idea Arthur Banning would not be fabulously wealthy; he would be fabulously poor! He would not be searching the world on an expensive yacht, searching for the woman of his dreams. No! It would be the other way around. The woman would search for him! Wow! What an idea! The woman would represent happiness; she would symbolize it, and Arthur Banning would symbolize all men. What an idea!

I started writing. But in a few minutes I was disgusted. I changed clothes and packed a suitcase. I needed a change in background. A great writer needed variation. When I finished packing I sat down and wrote a farewell note to my mother.

Dear Woman Who Gave Me Life:

The callous vexations and perturbations of this night have subsequently resolved themselves to a state which precipitates me, Arturo Bandini, into a brobdingnagian and gargantuan decision. I inform you of this in no uncertain terms. Ergo, I now leave you and your ever charming daughter (my beloved sister Mona) and seek the fabulous usufructs of my incipient career in profound solitude. Which is to say, tonight I depart for the metropolis to the east — our own Los Angeles, the city of angels. I entrust you to the benign generosity of your brother, Frank Scarpi, who is, as the phrase has it, a good family man (sic!). I am penniless but I urge you in no uncertain terms to cease your cerebral anxiety about my destiny, for truly it lies in the palm of the immortal gods. I have made the lamentable discovery over a period of years that living with you and Mona is deleterious to the high and magnanimous purpose of Art, and I repeat to you in no uncertain terms that I am an artist, a creator beyond question. And, per se, the fumbling fulminations of cerebration and intellect find little fruition in the debauched, distorted hegemony that we poor mortals, for lack of a better and more concise terminology, call home. In no uncertain terms I give you my love and blessing, and I swear to my sincerity, when I say in no uncertain terms that I not only forgive you for what has ruefully transpired this night, but for all other nights. Ergo, I assume in no uncertain terms that you will reciprocate in kindred fashion. May I say in conclusion that I have much to thank you for, O woman who breathed the breath of life into my brain of destiny? Aye, it is, it is.

Signed.

Arturo Gabriel Bandini.

Suitcase in hand, I walked down to the depot. There was a ten minute wait for the midnight train for Los Angeles. I sat down and began to think about the new novel.

§

JOHN FANTE was born in Colorado in 1909. He attended parochial school in Boulder, and Regis High School, a Jesuit boarding school. He also attended the University of Colorado and Long Beach City College.

Fante began writing in 1929 and published his first short story in *The American Mercury* in 1932. He published numerous stories in *The Atlantic Monthly, The American Mercury, The Saturday Evening Post, Collier's, Esquire,* and *Harper's Bazaar.* His first novel, *Wait Until Spring, Bandini* was published in 1938. The following year *Ask the Dust* appeared. (Both novels have been reprinted by Black Sparrow Press.) In 1940 a collection of his short stories, *Dago Red,* was published.

Meanwhile, Fante had been occupied extensively in screenwriting. Some of his credits include *Full of Life, Jeanne Eagels, My Man and I, The Reluctant Saint, Something for a Lonely Man, My Six Loves* and *Walk on the Wild Side.*

John Fante was stricken with diabetes in 1955 and its complications brought about his blindness in 1978, but he continued to write by dictation to his wife, Joyce, and the result was *Dreams from Bunker Hill* (Black Sparrow Press, 1982). He died at the age of 74 on May 8, 1983.

In 1985, Black Sparrow published Fante's selected stories, *The Wine of Youth,* and two early novels, which had never before been published, *The Road to Los Angeles* and *1933 Was a Bad Year.* In 1986 Black Sparrow brought out two previously unpublished novellas under the title *West of Rome. Full of Life* and *The Brotherhood of the Grape* were reprinted by Black Sparrow in 1988.

In 1989, Black Sparrow published *John Fante & H. L. Mencken: A Personal Correspondence 1930–1952,* and most recently in 1991 they published Fante's *Selected Letters 1932–1981.*